By KC BURN

NOVELS

Pen Name – Doctor Chicken

TORONTO TALES SERIES
Cop Out
Cover Up
Cast Off

Published by DREAMSPINNER PRESS
http://www.dreamspinnerpress.com

Pen Name –
Doctor Chicken
KC Burn

Dreamspinner Press

Published by
Dreamspinner Press
5032 Capital Circle SW
Suite 2, PMB# 279
Tallahassee, FL 32305-7886
USA
http://www.dreamspinnerpress.com/

This is a work of fiction. Names, characters, places, and incidents either are the product of author imagination or are used fictitiously, and any resemblance to actual persons, living or dead, business establishments, events, or locales is entirely coincidental.

Pen Name - Doctor Chicken
© 2013 KC Burn.

Cover Art
© 2013
Cover Art by Anne Cain.
annecain.art@gmail.com
Cover content is for illustrative purposes only and any person depicted on the cover is a model.

ISBN: 978-1-62798-384-6
Digital ISBN: 978-1-62798-383-9

Printed in the United States of America
First Edition
November 2013

Acknowledgments

Thanks as always to my super support group, Alex, Dottie, and Chudney. Also, thanks to Dolorianne, Lynn, Kiernan, and Tracy, who listened to me bitch and whine about this one.

Finally, thanks to Dreamspinner Press, who've been so good to me, and I'm glad they took a chance on this one.

One

"SO, WHAT are you into? Vanilla, bondage, fetish, gangbang? There's a bunch of places we could go. If we hit up Deviations before we go, we can grab any toys you want and still have time to get some... aids before the clubs open."

Stratford stuffed two jumbo shrimp in his mouth and tried not to choke because of Barry's unexpected questions. At least chewing prevented any necessity to reply right away.

When he'd agreed to go out with the cute young accountant from the real estate brokers in the same building where his own company was headquartered, he'd been thrilled. They'd flirted lightly for weeks, but Stratford had kept him at a distance. After all, he'd met Barry after he'd started seeing Nik. Then his relationship with Nik had imploded after he had met someone better than Stratford. He must have been giving off "available" vibes, because yesterday was the first time he'd ended up alone in the elevator with Barry, and Barry had immediately asked him out. And given him a promising grope.

Stratford had been even more thrilled with the plan when Barry had suggested they meet at Neptune's, one of the trendiest new seafood restaurants. Although he couldn't assume Barry was picking up the tab, he'd been courteous, and Stratford had been the envy of every gay man and straight woman they'd seen. Sure, they'd talked mostly about Barry, his job and life and friends, but that was okay. The parts of Stratford's life that weren't unbearably dull were pathetic or embarrassing. But he had high hopes for Barry. Until now, when they'd started discussing what they'd do after dinner.

For a first date, at least, one that didn't start in the bathroom stall at a club, Stratford had assumed they'd do something completely prosaic like a movie. Maybe a dance club. After all, he was getting to the point where he had to consider he had work the next morning and the fact that he needed to be mostly awake for it. What he hadn't expected was a frank and totally bizarre discussion of where they were going to get their freak on tonight. Apparently after picking up toys and aids.

Stratford wasn't a prude, but… okay, maybe he was a bit of prude. He'd slept with his fair share of guys, and he'd even had some heated hand jobs and blowjobs without sharing names either before, during, or after. But this was a date. He was getting a little old to plan an evening of debauchery with a man he didn't really know at all. Especially on a Thursday night.

On the other hand, he was getting tired of being alone all the time. After his best friend, Abby, moved in with her boyfriend, and he had a chance to watch how she and Thad interacted with each other, he realized he wanted that. He wanted someone in his life who was his, who would be there for him and whom he could build a life with.

After the Nik debacle, Stratford had high hopes it would be Barry, because he was getting tired of the depressing search. Barry had so many good qualities. He had a job and wasn't completely brain-dead. He didn't seem to be looking for a daddy. He seemed utterly normal and perfectly perfect. Stratford bit his lip to stop the alliteration, even if it occurred in the confines of his brain. He got more than enough of that at work, and he wasn't going to indulge on his own time.

After he'd chewed just about as long as he could without it appearing as though he had some sort of chewing disorder or had to chew each bite one hundred times, he swallowed. He had to say something.

"Er, well…."

"Hey, are you wearing a plug? If not, maybe we should get you one. Especially if we go to Q's. You want to be ready. Some of those guys are fucking hung."

An undignified and unmanly squeak escaped, and Stratford snuck a few sidelong glances at the other diners, wondering if they'd heard Barry. "Uh, no. I'm not. Wearing one, I mean." And he wasn't sure he wanted to go and buy one. Plugs were a little intimate, weren't they? After all, he'd found out a fair amount about Barry's life, but he hadn't even found out if the man had brothers or sisters yet, and Barry knew next to nothing about him. Had they truly progressed to a frank discussion of butt plugs?

Stratford took a deep breath. Maybe he hadn't found a man because he was a little too inhibited. At least when it came to dating. Certainly Nik had thought so. Maybe this was more normal than he'd expected. "So, are you… uh… wearing one?"

"Me? No, why would I? I don't bottom."

Stratford blinked. Somehow, in their abrupt conversational turn to sexual proclivities, Barry had assumed Stratford was some sort of power bottom, who, with the aid of his best friend, the always-present butt plug, would be willing to bottom not only for Barry but some random well-hung guys at an as-yet-undetermined club.

"What makes you think I do?"

Barry laughed, a sound Stratford might otherwise have likened to a burbling brook. Fuck. No more fucking alliteration! But the laugh just left him cold.

"Oh, Stratford. You've got a great sense of humor."

So, just because he was slim and liked wearing bow ties to work, he was automatically a bottom? And a subby one at that. What the fuck? He sometimes liked to top too. And there was more to sex than anal, anyway. Lots of things that he liked. The whole submissive thing wasn't him. Some of his decisions weren't well thought out, and he'd been accused of jumping in with both feet before checking to make sure he wasn't leaping off a cliff, especially when it came to men. But at least the decisions were all his own, good or bad. He also hated it when guys assumed bottom meant submissive, anyway. Not all sex, anal or otherwise, required submission.

Barry gave him a speculative glance, and even the bizarre discussion diminished his movie-star good looks.

"We can save the kinkier stuff for next week. There's a great BDSM night at Joey's next Saturday. But I've got a friend. He'll be at Q's tonight. You'd look awesome taking it from both ends. He's really hot too. I think Q's might be the best choice for tonight."

This time, Stratford couldn't avoid choking, and he grabbed at the nearly untouched glass of pinot grigio to clear the blockage in his throat. And yet, with Barry's bulging muscles—which had been cruelly obscured by his normal work attire—tousled hair, and flashing blue eyes, he couldn't quite bring himself to let go of the dream.

"What if it was just you and me for today?" Had Stratford been caught up so long in his stupid-ass career that he'd missed the gay memo that two guys together, no props or kink, had become passé and boring?

"Oh. Sure, yeah, if that's what you want." Barry wrinkled his nose a tiny bit but didn't seem too upset by Stratford's request.

Stratford let out a sigh of relief. He should be flattered, right? After all, if Barry had asked for a quickie in one of the public bathrooms in their office building, Stratford would have probably said yes. Maybe.

But Barry had to be attracted and interested. Otherwise there would have been no need for him to issue a dinner invitation. Which meant maybe Barry could be just as nervous as he was and as invested in the night going well. It was a little flattering, as well. There was no mistaking Barry's sexual interest. Stratford could work with that for now. As long as there wasn't any more discussion of plugs. At least not over dinner.

A club wasn't the best place to get to know someone, but a few hours dancing with Barry would set the stage for a second date after they both got off.

"ABBY, I swear, I'm never going to find my own Thad."

Stratford should have waited until he'd gotten home to call Abby, because the wind was going to freeze his fingers into a permanent curl around his phone. Gloves, scarfs, and wind-resistant fabrics hadn't suited his super-sexy Barry-bait outfit. Unfortunately, the Barry bait had been too enticing. Or the wrong kind of enticing. Sluts might wear shirts and pants as tight as his, but they didn't wear bow ties, did they? At least he was able to grab a latte on the way home. Aside from being one of his few expensive indulgences, it was keeping his left hand warmish.

"Of course you will. Are you sure you're not judging him too harshly? You sometimes have unrealistic expectations."

He snorted. No one had to know he'd had a sneaking little thought that he'd so dazzle Barry with his erudition and joie de vivre that the man would immediately become smitten and fall in love. Besides, Abby already knew he was a hopeless romantic.

"There was a certain romantic touch to the butt plug discussion over shrimp devolving into a dessert discussion on whether silicone, rubber, or glass was preferable for dildos. A dead giveaway, if I'd been paying attention. I mean, anyone who has enough information to write a dissertation on dildo production materials is either way too oversexed for me or hasn't had enough sex with other people... and probably for an excellent reason, as I discovered."

An older man in a fedora, walking in the opposite direction, gave Stratford a raised-brow look, and Stratford simply rolled his eyes and shrugged.

"Ford, you slut. You didn't! On a first date?" Abby's light, teasing tone hadn't the slightest hint of censure, but it could have. After all, Stratford had had his slutty moments, to be sure, but slutty wasn't the best way to snag a boyfriend. He didn't think. Or at least, not too slutty. What man didn't like a hint of slut? Monogamous slut. If there was such a thing.

"Uh, hello, you still there?"

"What, oh, yes. Sorry." Stratford had to stop drifting to his fantasies of a fairytale ending.

"You dog. You did it, didn't you? And how was it?"

"No. Really, I didn't. I mean, he blew me a little bit."

This time it was Abby who snorted. "Blew you a little bit? Kind of like being a little bit preggers, you know."

"It's never a good sign when you have to say 'watch the teeth,' followed closely by 'don't bite that.' Puts a damper on things."

"You think?" Loud gales of laughter buffeted him across the wireless waves, and Stratford pursed his lips. Why was his dating life such a fucking joke? Stupidly, though, he'd suffered through it, figuring Barry just hadn't had the right teacher, and Stratford found himself still auditioning for the role. Another gust of wind whipped past him, and he took a couple fortifying sips of his latte in the hopes of warding off the chill, but the cold air had leeched most of the heat from it.

Abby took a couple of gasping breaths before she spoke again. "Where exactly did you engage in the toothy oral sex? Surely not in the bathroom at Neptune?"

"Of course not. I have too much class for that." Stratford resolutely ignored the fresh chuff of laughter. "No, we ended up at Q's. We had a drink and, well...."

"That's when you finally gave him the heave-ho?"

"No, I left when he told me he'd signed us up for the amateur sex show."

This time he had to pull the phone away from his ear because Abby's shrieks of laughter pierced his eardrums.

"It's not that funny. Are you drunk?" But his questions didn't penetrate her whoops interspersed with heaving inhalations, and he didn't think telling her his dick still hurt would garner any sympathy whatsoever.

"I can't fucking breathe, you fucker," she wheezed at him. Served her fucking right for laughing at his misery. Barry could have been the one. If he hadn't been a deviant. Or too presumptuous.

"Abby, it's not funny. He didn't even ask!"

"And what, that would have made a difference?"

Stratford sniffed. "What sort of slut do you take me for? Sex in public isn't even a third-date activity." Or ever, really. He might be out-there gay and a wee bit singed from all his flaming, but he was far too skinny to be baring his bits in front of an audience.

The laughing continued. "Oh my fucking God, Ford. I gotta go."

"What?"

"Because I totally have to pee now."

"Oh for fuck's sake. Later." He let the call lapse, not as irritated as he pretended. One day, this might be a funny story, but for now, all he could focus on was his disappointment that the promise of his dream Barry had fallen so far short of real-life Barry. And the cruel disappointment that a bad blowjob was actually worse than no blowjob at all. Until tonight, he'd never have believed that possible. Sad to say, but Barry should have come with a warning label. A complete nonstarter in the relationship department.

Stratford would soon be thirty, and to have Barry, still in his early twenties, demonstrate such interest, had been a much bigger victory at the beginning of the evening than it was now.

Phone tucked safely away, Stratford adjusted himself and grimaced, hoping he wasn't going to have explain bite marks and a request for a rabies shot at the clinic. He was reasonably certain Barry hadn't punctured the condom, but he and a hand mirror were going to finish out the evening together, just to be sure.

Shaking the much lighter cardboard cup, he wasn't sure if it was worth drinking the last of it. Cold lattes didn't do it for him, and the weather had sucked most of the heat from the liquid.

He rounded the corner, the wind howling and whipping down the street, stirring the desiccated autumn leaves into a swirling frenzy. With a sigh, he approached the bus stop, glowing in small patch of light from the flickering overhead streetlight.

Although it had gotten dark before he'd met Barry for dinner, it was still too damn early to be heading home. And yet, Stratford wanted nothing more than a cup of hot chocolate, a warm bath, and a sci-fi book where all the shitty dates got turned into mindless android servants or got zapped by lasers for being bitey assholes. Failing that, he'd take a romantic thriller with a happy ending. If he couldn't have one of his own, he might as well enjoy a fictional one. He'd lost all energy and appetite for socializing and wasn't even interested in hanging out at his favorite cafe. At least Barry had paid for dinner.

Stratford shivered and stepped out into the street, searching for the distinctive lights of a city bus, but there was none to be seen. And at this particular intersection, he could see a fucking long way. He wrapped his arms around himself and checked the timetable posted below the red and white bus stop sign. Dammit. He'd just missed it. He'd been hoping for a cab home from Barry's place, not a damned bus after a disastrous date.

After a second's deliberation, he decided to start walking. At least that way he might not freeze to death, even if the walk was longer than he'd like in shoes that weren't much suited for hiking. With the windchill, he couldn't feel his toes, anyway, so he might as well take advantage of that. Good thing he'd decided he needed to get some direction in his life, because this was a stellar start.

THE next block, about halfway home, was fucking long, but an inviting yellow glow spilled out from the bank of windows at the community center. It almost looked warm, and Stratford edged closer to the building. Reflected light had to have some warmth, didn't it?

As soon as he approached, he glanced inside. The community center offered a variety of classes on a dizzying array of topics, all depending on who was willing to donate their time to teach the classes. Stratford had considered, more than once, taking a class in something, but the ones that interested him weren't the freebies. He already lived in a borderline illegal shithole apartment—no need to spend money for something where there wasn't even the prospect of getting laid.

This time, though, it wasn't a bunch of uncoordinated people wearing spandex or reciting simple sentences in other languages. In fact, he wasn't sure he'd ever seen this particular room in use when he'd walked past. It was a large kitchen area, and Stratford hadn't even realized it was used for anything besides catering low-budget parties and receptions in the center's "ballroom."

A cooking class. Stratford stepped up close to the window, a hair's breadth away from pressing his nose against the glass. He hadn't had a proper home-cooked meal since his parents booted him out of their lives when he was nineteen. Abby had saved his life back then, but a cook she wasn't, and none of the boyfriends he'd had in the meantime had ever cooked for him. Assuming any of them could. It was one reason why he'd kept making excuses for Barry's behavior. Barry had taken him to a nice restaurant. Stratford spent so much time scrimping and saving that he appreciated the value of a good meal, and Neptune had more than lived up to its reputation for serving excellent meals.

Peering in, he tried to determine what they were cooking. It might have been Italian, but he wasn't entirely sure he'd recognize the ingredients for anything.

A tall man in a deep-red dress shirt and black tailored slacks walked across the room. Stratford's heart rate ramped up as everyone else in the room dimmed. Now, there was a dish he'd like to sample, and he did look Italian. The dress shirt fit an impressive chest and biceps as though it were also tailored. The elevated preparation tables obscured a view of the man's package, but Stratford didn't care. Thick, dark hair framed a face that was so damn regal it could convince anyone to sin. Olive skin, a clean-shaven square jaw just starting to reveal a shadow of where the facial hair would grow in, and presumably brown eyes. Stratford couldn't see at this distance, but he assumed the guy's eyes would be brown, and he really wanted to know what flavor. Dark like his hair or light like cognac? Stratford pressed himself against the glass, trying to get closer.

The man rounded one of the tables and smiled down at his petite female partner. The smile, even in profile, was devastating to the senses, and Stratford shivered. Was the woman his wife? Girlfriend? It was too much to hope for that he'd be gay, but then again, a guy like that was so far out of Stratford's league he might as well be an alien.

Completely losing interest in what they were cooking, Stratford stayed and watched, unable to rip his gaze from the guy, even if all he saw was a well-formed back and the occasional glimpse of a profile models would pay money for. Every time his hand moved, Stratford tried to catch sight of his ring finger. Not that a lack of wedding band meant anything, but its presence would mean something.

After a few minutes' observation, it was clear that his guy... the guy... wasn't in a long-term relationship with the girl at his side. There were too many awkward moments, too many near hits when they moved around each other, but the girl's adoring looks meant she was interested, even if this was only a date.

Growing more and more irritated by the blonde's continual "accidental" touches to the guy's arm, back, and hand, Stratford looked for any sign of interest from the hot, hot man.

For every touch Blondie made, Italian guy merely moved out of reach. He didn't flinch away or look disgusted. In fact, Blondie usually got a sweet smile for her troubles, but he never touched her back and made sure any touch she initiated was fleeting. Didn't mean the man was gay, and didn't mean he wasn't on a date with Blondie, but it was enough to give Stratford hope.

Then, for no apparent reason, Italian guy turned fully around, staring right at Stratford, and he frowned. Like he'd been caught red-handed with his pants down, Stratford leapt back from the window, heart pounding. He turned and sprinted a few steps.

His feet caught a rough patch of sidewalk, and, unable to catch himself, the coffee cup went flying as he went down, hands first and knees a jarring, painful second.

The pain was enough to bring him to his senses. How long had he been staring in that window? He was certain the Italian guy had seen him, and he'd been too close to the window to assume he'd been masked by darkness, but the Italian guy's sudden attention had startled him.

He stood and brushed off his hands. Blood oozed sluggishly from a few scrapes, and his knees throbbed. Fuck. Flexing his fingers, he cursed how tight and numb they felt. Italian guy had been so entrancing, Stratford had almost given himself hypothermia.

Another gust of wind blasted down the street, and this time, the full-body shakes had nothing to do with sexy men. His teeth chattered and the scrapes on his palms burned. A familiar sound hit his ears. Groaning, he turned to see a bus approaching. Frantically, he twisted his head, searching for a bus stop, but he was firmly in between stops.

Fuck.

The bus lumbered past him, and Stratford considered sitting down on the pavement and sobbing. Instead, he took a few breaths and limped along his way. It was only another ten blocks home. He could make it. But he had to get out of this wind. He made a right turn onto a small residential street to follow a tree-lined and somewhat less freezing path toward his apartment.

"GOODNESS, you're very skilled at stuffing those manicotti."

Vinnie Giani blinked at the suggestive tone in those words and darted a glance over his shoulder at his cooking partner. Bethany smiled at him with all the innocence of an angel; he must have imagined it. The woman was certainly pretty, but he had no interest in stuffing her manicotti. At all.

"Uh, thanks. My mother taught me." And he could make manicotti in his sleep.

"Did she?" Bethany smiled and patted his arm.

Despite the sweet innocence of Bethany's demeanor, he swore that every word out of his mouth only made him more enticing, like an ice cream sundae with an ever-increasing variety of toppings. If only he could completely ignore her, but being unintentionally annoying was no reason for rudeness on his part.

"So, Vincent, if your mother taught you how to do this—and I think it's awesome that you know how to cook—why are you taking this class?" Bethany tried to shove the ricotta cheese and spinach mixture into the slippery pasta tube and mangled it beyond recognition. Vinnie refrained from commenting on her technique.

"Because Italian is all I know how to cook." He knew almost all of the recipes his mother did, based on years of helping her feed his younger siblings, but as much as he loved cooking his mother's recipes, he also liked variety in his diet. The Cooking Around The World course seemed like a good place to start. He was only a little miffed they'd started the four-week, eight-class course with Italy. Or at least, started the actual cooking part with Italy. Tuesday's class didn't count because they hadn't done much more than learn basic terminology and cooking implements, which he could have skipped.

Bethany giggled. "Obviously, I don't know how to cook Italian, either. But I've always wanted to learn. Does your girlfriend cook?"

Vinnie tried to glance at his watch, but the bare skin on his wrist reminded him he'd taken it off prior to starting class. The classroom

11

had a large clock hanging above the instructor's workstation, and it told him there was still half a class left. Bethany could very well have been asking about his girlfriend as an innocent means to make conversation, but she'd already touched his arm and shoulder too often for it to be completely platonic. He sighed. He generally wasn't a fan of telling people he'd just met that he was gay, mostly because he didn't think it was their business, but he'd spent long enough pretending. As soon as he'd come out, he found he didn't have the stomach to let a woman think for a minute there was a chance he'd ask her out.

"Nope, no girlfriend." No boyfriend, either, but he had hopes. Now that his sister Marissa had finally gotten her MBA and taken on some of the heavy lifting at the company, for the first time since high school Vinnie had the time to find a boyfriend. Not that he hadn't had his share of one-night stands or even the occasional rent boy, but dating took time, time he'd never had before while first trying to keep his mother and sisters fed, and then later, while trying to make a go of his business.

He had no fucking idea how to go about finding a boyfriend, and after hiring Marissa, he had far more time on his hands than he'd hoped. His mom had always told him cooking was going to help him find a nice girl... until he came out and she switched genders when giving him advice. So far, it hadn't happened, but he looked forward to being able to cook for a boyfriend or husband one day.

"Wife?" Bethany's expression turned predatory.

"No wife. We'd better get these in the oven if they're going to be cooked in time." Vinnie shoved the dish at Bethany. "Be back in a minute. I just have to make a phone call."

He sped out into the hall, and to satisfy his conscience, he pulled out his phone and checked his e-mail. A couple of work e-mails he could put off until the morning and a spam e-mail for a dating site. A grimace curled his lips. Putting his information into a dating site seemed like a recipe for disaster. For all the success of his company, he wasn't rich. Well-off, yes, but not rich. He'd already fended off a number of people—men and women—who had hopes of getting a free ride from him in return for a few blowjobs. He might be new to the world of dating, but he'd had to grow up damn fast during his teen years, and he wasn't stupid. It wasn't difficult to spot that sort of insincerity.

But he couldn't stay out in the hallway forever, and while the manicotti cooked, they were supposed to be preparing an antipasto plate. No desserts, unfortunately. Desserts were reserved for the last two classes.

"I THOUGHT you'd got lost out there." Bethany touched his arm again and giggled. "Ready for the antipasto?"

Vinnie smiled and took a small step away. "Sure thing."

Next week, he was going to try to team up with a different partner. A few people were taking the class as twosomes, but there were enough who weren't that surely one of them would be happy to take Bethany off his hands.

The instructor began offering a few tips and related information, but Vinnie stopped listening.

Something was different. He glanced around the room. Then he spun around. A man stood at the window, staring inside, but he disappeared a split second later.

He nudged Bethany. "Did you see that?"

"See what?"

"I thought I saw a guy at the window."

She shrugged. "You might have. People probably look in here all the time. Especially vagrants."

"I don't think it was a vagrant." The glimpse of the guy he'd seen had been quite thin, but Vinnie could have sworn he'd seen a dress shirt, a jacket, and a bow tie. Vagrants didn't wear bow ties, did they? With the cold weather, they were usually puffy with layers of raggedy clothing. If this guy had been a vagrant, he was really new at the job. In fact, he thought the guy might have been young.

"Wouldn't be a surprise, would it? Looking in at all this food."

Vinnie stared down at their table. "I'll be back in a minute."

He grabbed the loaf of crusty bread and wrapped it in a paper towel. If there was a vagrant out there salivating over their bounty, he was going to at least offer him the loaf of bread.

"Where are you going?" Bethany's voice had become shrill and whiny.

Vinnie didn't bother to answer.

Out on the street, a vicious wind sliced through the thin fabric of his dress shirt. A terrible night to be homeless. He glanced up and down the street, but aside from the retreating lights of the city bus, there was no one outside.

Shrugging, he went back inside, determined to fend off the ham-handed advances of Miss Bethany.

STRATFORD needed two hands to get his key in the lock of the back door of his building, and when he finally forced the key to turn with fingers he could barely feel, he stumbled inside. The stairway up to the second floor was dimly lit by a single bare bulb. He dreaded the day it burnt out because he'd probably kill himself if he tried to change it, and his landlord would undoubtedly not care.

Right now, though, the biggest hurdle was getting up those stairs. He groaned. So close and he could finally shut the door on this shitbag of a night.

He eyed the grubby floor. It was warm and out of the wind; he could maybe just curl up on the cracked linoleum and sleep. Better than most homeless people had it.

A muffled meow made him sigh. He'd been so flustered trying to find the perfect outfit he hadn't fed Bob before he'd left on his date. Not that Bob didn't have crunchies to eat, but he really liked the canned food. Guilt pushed him to lift his legs and clamber up the stairs like an old man with rheumatism.

At the top of the stairs, feeling returned to his feet and fingertips. With a stifled cry of anguish, he had to use two hands—again—to get his key in the lock of his apartment door.

Bob nearly tripped him as he lurched through the door.

"Bob. What the hell? It's not like you're starving." In fact, the cat probably needed to go on a diet, but considering the way he'd inherited Bob, he didn't have the heart to deny the fat tortoiseshell cat anything he wanted. Bob had been rejected every bit as much as Stratford had. Even if Bob's black-and-orange fur managed to show up on whatever color clothing he wore. There was no color Stratford could wear that would camouflage the hair.

Insanely loud rumbles filled the tiny, half-assed kitchen as his mottled black-and-orange tub of lard twined around his legs as he scooped out a serving of food.

Grimacing, he flexed his fingers before putting the can in the fridge. A dull ache throbbed in his palms, matched by an equal flare of pain in his knees. He poured himself a glass of water before hobbling to the bathroom to run a bath.

He stared at his hands before he started to undress. His hands must have been number than he'd thought because they were a lot bloodier than he'd realized. Gingerly, he undressed, but at least he was wearing dark colors—the blood wouldn't ruin his second-best outfit. It might still manage to bait someone better than Barry the Biter.

"Fuck." No lint brush in the world was going to save the ripped knees of his pants. His knees were as scraped and bloodied as his hands and were going to bruise. Best date ever! Lip curling in disgust, he lowered his battered body into the warm, sudsy water.

Hissing as the water hit his scrapes, he remembered his hands and knees might not be the only skin broken. But the soap didn't sting his dick, thank God. He might have cried if his dick was damaged. Leaning back against the chilly tub, he thought of the only thing that was any good at all about the evening: Italian guy. Blood pumped lazily into his groin as he pictured what a convenient height those prep-work cooking tables were for bending over and….

He curled his fingers, ready to take himself in hand and realized stroking off was going to hurt. This time he focused on trying to remember what Italian guy had been making in class. It didn't take long to realize he hadn't paid any attention to the food, too intent on the peach of an ass in black dress pants. For now, the lazy throb in his groin was undemanding, but if he didn't stop his mind from stripping down that gorgeous hunk and trying to imagine what sort of equipment he was packing, he'd end up with blue balls.

What he needed to do was figure out how he was going to face Barry tomorrow at work.

Ah. Instant libido killer.

Two

STRATFORD shut his apartment door behind him and sighed. It had been a long fucking day, and all he wanted was to curl up in the fetal position.

He shrugged out of his winter jacket and stripped off his emerald bow tie, tossing them both over a hook on the wall. At least the office dress code only insisted on either tie or suit jacket, not both. He didn't know how he'd be able to work if he had to wear a suit jacket all day. But then, he didn't know how he'd gotten stuck in this crappy dead-end job for so long, either. The mysteries of the universe were inexplicable.

Friday afternoons at the office sucked. It never failed. His boss, Mr. Gonzalez, always seemed to start his weekend early whenever Stratford was swamped, but invariably hung around the office all afternoon when things were slow, thereby forcing Stratford to pretend he was busy until five fucking o'clock. Unexpectedly, his tumble yesterday had resulted in stiff, achy muscles that hurt even worse than they had last night, and he'd wanted nothing more than to go home and watch TV with a tumbler full of cheap booze. Maybe he'd even break out some porn.

Grimacing, he flexed his hands and decided they probably weren't up to the job today, either. The day had been made immeasurably more stressful because he'd also had to be on the lookout for Barry. After ditching the guy last night, he wasn't much up for any awkward elevator confrontation. He'd even started work an hour early and took the stairs—all sixteen flights—when he left, just to

17

ensure he avoided the guy. Perhaps not the nicest route, but he truly didn't know how to deal with Barry at the workplace. Not when he knew what he knew. Maybe he should thank the guy for showing his true self so early so there was never a chance for a relationship blowout like he'd had with Nik. Or even worse, the horrific ending to his relationship with Ian.

The strident tones of an old-fashioned telephone made him jump before he scrabbled to retrieve his phone from his jacket pocket.

"Hey there," Abby crowed as soon as Stratford answered. "We decided to have a barbecue tomorrow, since the weather's supposed to be good."

Stratford snorted. Yes, perhaps the weather was supposed to be good for November, but it was still November. Thad had some sort of overdeveloped meat-searing gene. He'd heard tales of the man barbecuing in the snow, but had never been invited to a midwinter barbecue, thank all the powers in the universe. The very thought itself made him shudder as though he were hip deep in drifts this second.

"Good for you." At the sound of his voice, Bob's head poked out of his bedroom, where he'd undoubtedly nested under Stratford's comforter. For a fat fifteen-pounder, Bob was rather delicate about the cold, and if the wind came from the east, it whipped right through his inadequately sealed kitchen window, dropping the temperature several degrees.

"You're going to come, right?"

For a second or two, he considered lying about having to work on the weekend, but Abby would not only know, she'd be pissed.

Instead, he chose the truth, even though Abby wouldn't be any happier about hearing it. "Honestly, I don't know. I'm so beat right now, I can't imagine wanting to leave the apartment at all this weekend."

Stratford moved into the kitchen, Bob eagerly rubbing against his legs, encouraging him to hurry the fuck up with the canned food.

"You aren't still depressed about that date with Jaws, are you?"

"No, I'm not." *Liar.* "And thanks, Abby, now I'll have to be careful not to call him that when I see him next."

"Please. I know you're going to avoid him like he's diseased until you think he's forgotten about the whole thing."

"I'm not." Was he?

"You hate confrontation like I've never seen. Going out to clubs with you is like some crazy sitcom as you duck from ex-boyfriends and ex-fucks."

Stratford drew in a shocked breath, not sure how to deal with this sudden attack. His heart rate sped up as he considered just hanging up and turning off his phone for the rest of the weekend. He wasn't that bad, was he?

"Shit." Abby's voice softened. "Ford, honey, I'm sorry."

He still couldn't quite bring himself to speak.

"Ford, are you still there? I didn't mean it. Well, I did, in a way. You don't like confrontation, and I know why you don't, but you gotta remember, it was one date. We all have had shitty dates. You buck up and move on. I know you had dreams about this guy being the one."

Stratford finally found his voice, although it was quieter than normal. "Stupid, right?"

"No, honey, no. You want to find someone and that's good. That's okay. Pinning your hopes on a guy you've never spent time with was maybe… premature. Have you thought about signing up for a dating service? That way your options would be restricted to other guys who want the same thing. Have the same interests."

Abby wasn't talking about hookup sites, and while Stratford had used them occasionally when he was desperate, they weren't his thing. He also wasn't sure about dating services, either. Too clinical, and could an algorithm guide you to love? Love was more visceral and ephemeral, wasn't it? Be nice if he knew for sure, because trying to bend himself into pretzels to please a guy who was only going kick him to the curb or screw him over couldn't be fucking love.

"I'll think about it." He would too. After all, he wasn't having too much luck finding a guy on his own. Or at least, one he didn't mind being around and who didn't mind being around him.

"You need someplace other than work and clubs to meet decent guys, Ford. What about taking a course?"

"Well, that would cost money, Abby." The singsong reply probably didn't soften the sarcasm. He'd be paying off student loans for at least another three years, and she knew it. That didn't give him a whole lot of leeway for frivolous expenses.

"It could be an investment in your future, Ford." Abby had no difficulty slinging his mocking sarcasm right back. Which was only one of many reasons he loved her. "Get you the fuck out of that shit job."

Stratford sighed. The job was shit. It was only supposed to be temporary until he got his graphic novel off the ground. But he hadn't anticipated how expensive a four-year degree would be when he started with nothing. Less than nothing. He hadn't anticipated how much of his income would be eaten up by repaying those loans. Food. Electricity. Any classes that would help him get a better job would take a lot of time and probably more money than he had. But a class wasn't a terrible idea.

"I could maybe take a cooking class."

"You? Take a cooking class? You've got a hot plate and a microwave and three square feet of counter space. The last time you made me boxed mac & cheese you served it in a Pyrex measuring cup. What would be the point?"

That hurt. He wasn't going to be in this shit apartment forever. He'd better not be. "Hey, I could learn to cook."

"Sure, yeah, why don't you start by coming over tomorrow and helping Thad barbecue?"

"Nice try, Abby. Seriously, I fell yesterday on the way home, and I'm a little stiff."

"Ford! Why didn't you say something? Are you okay?"

"Yes, yes, just my normal clumsiness."

"You sure you don't want to come over? You could come over now, stay the night. Just like old times. Let me take care of you." Abby's voice had softened, the same tone he'd heard from the first time they'd met. That first year, Stratford had needed Abby to take care of him. But after that first year, he vowed to do it on his own, and he had, more or less. Right now, he wasn't sure he wanted to subject himself to

Abby's happy home life with her boyfriend. That might hurt just too damned much.

He softened the edge in his own voice. "I'll be fine. I'll have a *Doctor Who* marathon."

Abby's eye rolling was loud and clear in her snicker. "You have fun with that. Don't beat off too much."

Stratford sucked in a gasp in mock offense, but Abby had already disconnected. As if he knew Stratford was off the phone, Bob let out a tiny, high-pitched meow, which was at complete odds with the size of the chubby fur ball.

"Yes, yes. I'm getting it."

With Bob fed, Stratford checked his fridge and his solitary pantry cupboard. Both of which were alarmingly bare, aside from a half a bag of potato chips and a full bottle of wine. He shrugged. He'd eaten worse meals. Tomorrow would be soon enough to replenish, sometime in the midst of his beloved *Doctor Who* marathon. After, of course, he fired up his laptop and checked out the available cooking classes at the community center.

VINNIE grimaced. The sounds of dishes and utensils clanging together illustrated how late he was. He'd intended to come early, try to scope out a non-Bethany partner. A shudder passed through him at the similarities to high school, trying to jockey for a coveted science partner. Then again, Bethany might have given up on him showing up and set her sights on some other poor bastard. If only Bethany had been a cute, single gay guy he might not have been so hesitant.

Squaring his shoulders, he walked into the room. There were two stations that had only one person standing at them, and he made a beeline for the one that didn't have Bethany waving like a lunatic. A thin young guy, face obscured by a hank of wavy brown hair, stood poking at utensils as though they might bite, but Vinnie didn't mind a complete novice.

"Need a partner?"

The guy lifted his head, eyes almost panicked. Vinnie's knees wobbled, and he grabbed the edge of the table for support. The guy wasn't nearly as young as he'd thought at first. Late twenties, maybe thirty. But the shaggy, ear-length hair hid a face so gorgeous it stole Vinnie's ability to breathe.

"Uh, yeah." Then the guy's eyes widened, and a dark-red flush raced up his neck to stain sharp, prominent cheekbones. The bow tie was adorable, but Vinnie bit back the urge to say that. Calling a guy cute might not make him a friend. He remembered the guy who'd stared in at the window last week. Was this him?

There was no guarantee the guy was gay, but Vinnie was a lot happier about spending time with this guy. He just had to make sure he didn't become this guy's Bethany. Because that would be beyond embarrassing.

Swallowing back the shock at his sudden, fierce attraction to this stranger, Vinnie stretched out a hand.

"I'm Vinnie." Except for a few years during high school where he'd gone by Vince, he was Vinnie to friends and family and Vincent to everyone else. Introducing himself as Vinnie only reinforced how much he wanted to get to know his new cooking partner.

"Hi. Um. I'm Stratford." His whiskey-brown gaze darted around the room, continually landing back to meet Vinnie's eyes.

"Stratford. Nice to meet you." Vinnie rounded the table, washed his hands, and turned back to Stratford. He spied a cardboard cup with the name of a nearby coffee shop he'd heard of but never been to. "Good coffee?"

"Yes. Well, it's a latte."

"Still coffee. I've heard good things about that place. Independent place, right?"

Stratford nodded. "It's my favorite." He took a hurried sip, as though he was afraid he'd revealed something he shouldn't. Vinnie merely concentrated on the bob of Stratford's Adam's apple as he swallowed. Vinnie licked his lips, concerned he might say or do something he shouldn't.

"What are we cooking today?"

"Pad Thai." From Stratford's expression, they might have been threatened with death if they failed.

"Cool. I love Thai food."

Stratford nodded, but continued to poke at the utensils as though they were Martian weaponry.

"I take it you've never made Thai food before." That had a nicer sound than *have you ever set foot inside a kitchen before.*

"No. No. I'm not much of a cook." Stratford cleared his throat. "What about you?"

Vinnie scanned the instructions posted at the front of the room and began preparations. "Well, I'm great with Italian, but not much else. That's why I'm here."

Quickly assessing their different skill levels, Vinnie divvied up the tasks, keeping the more advanced ones for himself. Even then, he needed to guide Stratford through a few basics, since he'd missed the first week.

They worked in silence for a few minutes while Vinnie wracked his brains for a way to ask if Stratford swung his way—and was single—without sounding as obvious as Bethany.

"At least we don't have to devein the shrimp." Vinnie had hated it the one time he'd done it, and Stratford was skittish enough that deveining shrimp might scare him away for good.

"Um… what's that?" Stratford held a few stalks of green onions in a tight fist.

Vinnie explained, hoping the explanation wasn't going to accomplish the same thing.

"Ew. Really?" The corner of Stratford's plush upper lip lifted in disgust, and he tapped at the bowl holding the raw, already deveined shrimp. Then Stratford looked at him, an impish smile on his face. "Draining the main vein, eh?"

Vinnie sputtered out a laugh, not sure how to deal with the sudden, sharp jolt of lust combined with the unexpected humor. There was a strong personality hiding under the shy glances and clumsy but gorgeous exterior; Vinnie wanted to see more.

Stratford smiled back at him, and Vinnie thought he might lose his mind if Stratford wasn't available and gay. Not that he'd had much opportunity to break out his gaydar, but odds were good that Stratford was gay. He'd wait until the end of the class, then ask Stratford out for a drink. Stratford's reaction should give him a clue if something a little more date-like would be appreciated.

Vinnie put the wok on to heat, then turned to Stratford, feeling they'd broken the ice. He tweaked Stratford's bow tie. "What's with the bow tie? I noticed it last week—that was you looking in the window, right?"

He had a split second to regret giving so much away before he knew for certain whether Stratford played on his team when the dark-red blush returned and Stratford fumbled, knocking a bunch of utensils clattering to the floor. Stratford tried to clutch at the cutlery cascade while Vinnie busied himself making sure the wok didn't overturn and nothing caught fire in the flames of the gas burner. He turned to tease Stratford, only to find him staring in horror at his hand, bright red with blood.

"Jeez, what happened?" He didn't wait for Stratford to respond. In one swift move, he turned off the burner and grabbed a towel to wrap around Stratford's hand.

"I think… I grabbed a knife." The flush had faded so completely, Stratford looked more ghost than man.

"Okay, okay. Here. Sit down for a moment." The workstations were equipped with stools, although it was usually easier to cook from a standing position. He kept the pressure on Stratford's palm and guided him to the seat. With gentle fingers, he grabbed Stratford's elbow and lifted, raising Stratford's hand above shoulder level.

The instructor had made her way to them, realizing there was a problem. Vinnie knew it all happened in a matter of seconds, minutes at most, but it somehow felt a whole lot longer.

"Are we okay?" Then she spied the bloodstained fabric around Stratford's hand. "Oh, no. Stratford."

"I think I should take him to the hospital, get him looked at. I didn't see how deep it was, but even if it's not too deep, a cut across the palm can affect a number of tendons." Vinnie made sure he kept a firm grip on Stratford's makeshift pressure bandage.

"I'll cancel class and take him."

"No, no. No sense in ruining everyone's session. I don't mind taking him." His family was incredibly accident-prone, and this would hardly be the first time he'd taken someone to the hospital.

"Where's the closest emergency department?"

"There's an urgent care walk-in, just on the other side of the building. It's still open, you might get him seen that much sooner. In fact, depending on where you parked, it might even be faster to walk."

"Thanks." Vinnie turned his attention to Stratford. "You think you can keep the pressure on this while we walk a little ways?"

Those sweet brown eyes were wide and possibly not comprehending Vinnie's question. Shit. This was going to be fucking awkward, trying to keep the pressure on while he guided Stratford around the building. Especially if he suddenly became faint.

One of the women from the next table, who Vinnie had pegged the first day as a schoolteacher or a soccer mom, came over lugging an enormous tapestry purse. "Here. This might help."

In another life, Vinnie might have been embarrassed that he had no trouble recognizing the slim, plastic-covered square, but he'd used maxi pads as pressure bandages more than once in the past.

"That's great, but I'll need some string or something to keep the pressure on."

Soccer mom was still rummaging, and seconds later, pulled out a roll of duct tape. "I knew this was in here."

Vinnie raised an eyebrow and gave her an admiring nod before quickly exchanging the towel bandage for a duct tape and maxi pad one.

"Okay, let's go. Try to keep your hand above your shoulder." He tucked Stratford into his side, grabbed both their jackets with his free hand, and led Stratford out.

The instructor followed and held open the door. "If you aren't back by the time class ends, I'll meet you over there. Thank you, Vincent."

"No problem." As soon as the chilly November evening hit them, Stratford pressed himself closer to Vinnie. Vinnie only hoped he'd have a chance to experience this again, without the blood or injury, because Stratford had caught his interest but good.

THE cold night air helped numb both the throbbing in Stratford's hand and the humiliation in his brain, but as soon as Vinnie helped him into the urgent care clinic, both made themselves known again, vying for his attention. He wrinkled his nose. The smell of antiseptic and sick people was a far cry from the warm cooking scents that had begun to fill up the classroom when they'd left.

"You can go, I'll be okay," Stratford said. Aside from the fact he wanted to bawl like a baby, he'd be okay. Way to make a good impression on a guy.

"Don't be ridiculous. I don't mind waiting, and maybe I can keep your mind off things until the doctor can see you." Vinnie guided him to a seat.

Stratford's hands were never going to forgive him. Nor would his dick, because—just his luck—he'd managed to cut the hand he used for jacking off. If he thought the bruising and scrapes from the other day were too uncomfortable for beating off, he didn't want to know how bad it would be with stitches.

"Thank you." Vinnie was not only sexy but nice. It wasn't Vinnie's fault that a little twitch of his bow tie, in a gesture that had surprised him by its intimacy, had sparked Stratford into being his spastic, clumsy self. So cool, so sexy to find himself in urgent care, injured, covered in blood and shrimp juice, wrapped in duct tape and…. "What's this bandage thingy?"

"Maxi pad."

Vinnie's voice was matter-of-fact enough to cut through Stratford's shock and at least kept him from flinging his hand around like a cat with wet paws.

"Relax. That's what it's made for. It's clean and absorbent and has to have less bacteria than a community center dish towel."

Stratford inspected the bandage while Vinnie retrieved a clipboard with a form on it. It wasn't as terrifying as he imagined, although he wasn't sure why it was so oddly shaped. However, he resolutely refused to think about what flap went where.

Vinnie handed him the clipboard, then frowned. "Let me guess. You're right-handed."

"Uh, yeah."

A smile made the corners of Vinnie's eyes crinkle. "Then I guess it's a good thing I stuck around. Where's your wallet? I'll start filling this out for you."

Okay, yes, the day could get more humiliating. Surprise! "My wallet's in my right back pocket."

"I know it's not funny, but man." Vinnie shook his head. "Is your luck always this bad?"

"So it seems." Stratford wasn't about to tell this guy it was all his fault. He still hadn't decided if the guy was gay, and he didn't want to freak him out if he was straight. They might both be in the six-foot range for height, but Vinnie was broader and way more muscular. There was no doubt in Stratford's mind that Vinnie could wipe the floor with him, and Stratford was further hindered by the gaping wound on his hand and still-bruised knees.

"Right, stand up."

Before Stratford had stretched up to his full height, a minor pressure at his backside alerted him to Vinnie's plan. His battered black wallet was in Vinnie's hand, and it had happened so fast, he hadn't even gotten to enjoy the near grope. His lower lip pooched out a bit, and he sank back in the chair. For a moment, he forgot about his injury, but his careless drop into his seat jarred his hand, and he hissed as the dull throb morphed into a sharp stab of teeth-clenching pain.

"Hey, hey, careful. I think you're up next, but we don't want you to bleed out before the doctor sees you."

Bleed out? Stratford stared at his hand, peering at the gaps between the duct tape, searching for evidence he was bleeding through the makeshift bandage. He hadn't thought the cut had been quite that deep.

"Relax." Vinnie laid a large, warm hand on his knee. "I was kidding. I'm sorry, I shouldn't have said that. You're going to be fine."

Letting out his sudden panic with a long, relieved exhalation, Stratford relaxed back into the chair and watched as Vinnie deftly flipped through his wallet for the appropriate information.

27

"Stratford Dale. That's an interesting name. Is Stratford a family name?" Vinnie didn't look up but continued scratching a pen across the form, creating legible letters with short, precise strokes.

Cradling his arm, because holding his hand above his shoulder was starting to ache like a bitch, Stratford wondered what circle of hell involved a sweet, sexy straight man taking care of you when you were in a bind from being an infatuated moron.

"No. I was apparently conceived on my parents' road trip in England." He sighed. Sometimes he thought about changing his name. Whenever he talked about how he got his name, he was forcibly reminded that the parents who had so whimsically named him no longer considered him their son.

"Road trip?" Vinnie looked up from the form. "How do they know you were specifically conceived in Stratford?"

He let out a bitter laugh. "They don't. They just picked a name they liked from their trip. It could be worse, I suppose. I mean, have you seen a map of England? I'm lucky they didn't call me Basingstoke or Ipswich."

Vinnie laughed, and Stratford melted just a little bit more as the cheery sound seemed to caress him.

"Yes, I suppose that's true. Or they could have been touring Wales."

Stratford blinked. Welsh names were kinda cool looking, but he'd rather have one he could pronounce. "Huh. Never even occurred to me."

"Ever been there?" Vinnie bent back to his task, his voice abstracted.

"Wales? No. I'd like to one day." He'd like to go just about anywhere, but since his stupid job paid peanuts and his loans were still hanging over his head, even a bus trip to Vegas was out of his reach for at least the next three years.

"Yeah, me too."

"Stratford Dale?" A nurse in yellow scrubs called his name, but he and Vinnie were—amazingly—the only ones in the waiting room. Eight o'clock on a Tuesday must be a slow night for emergencies. He was thankful, though. He wasn't sure how much longer he could stand the slice of fire on his palm. What if he couldn't work? He couldn't remember what kind of disability coverage he had, and if there was even the tiniest loophole, he was certain Gonzalez would find a way to fire him.

"Good timing. I just finished." Vinnie handed him the clipboard. "I'll be here when you get done."

"You don't have to. I can take a cab or something." Yeah, like he was going to fork over the bucks for a cab. He'd grab the bus; the stop wasn't that far away.

"No, I don't mind, and it's probably safer if you have someone watching out for you until you get home, especially if they give you painkillers."

Walking home in the cold wasn't going to kill him, but he was glad Vinnie was staying. He'd probably change his mind once his hand stopped hurting, but for now he was glad not to be alone.

VINNIE glanced at his watch. They'd taken Stratford very quickly, but he'd had enough experience with injuries to know Stratford might have had to wait a long time if it weren't a ghost town in here. The cut needed stitches but wasn't critical. People always told him that boys were rambunctious and crazy, but when his sisters were kids, they'd been wild things. Wilder things—his sisters weren't docile or demure. Broken bones, gouges, burns, split chins and later on, a few trips for alcohol poisoning scares. He'd seen it all and been the one to take the injured girl to the hospital while his mom stayed home and looked after the other two. He much preferred blood to puke, but he was an old hand at dealing with both.

He was still a little worried about Stratford's hand, but he was a lot happier being the one to bring him to aid. His sisters accused him all the time of being a controlling old nana, but he couldn't help it. He'd been taking care of his family since he was eighteen, and he couldn't help but want to take care of Stratford. Their age difference wasn't much—at thirty-four, Vinnie had no more than five or six years on him—but there was something about Stratford that called to him. The clumsiness and flustered embarrassment brought out his protective instincts, and that's all he'd be willing to say aloud.

Deep in the depths of himself, he could admit that Stratford's lanky body, large, expressive brown eyes, and mop of brown hair got him fucking hot. The bow tie quirk was just another mystery he wanted to unravel, preferably while he was unraveling Stratford out of tie and shirt and pants. Was it too selfish to keep to his plan to ask Stratford out? Was there some gay etiquette he was unaware of that governed asking out recently injured men?

For the first time in a long time, he wanted—badly—something for himself. He was looking forward to getting to know Stratford. Then again, he had five more cooking classes to get to know Stratford. He didn't have to rush things. God knew he warned his sisters about letting a man go too fast. Probably he should practice what he preached. At least he'd never preached abstinence. His mother might believe that his sisters, except for Gabriella, were still virgins, but Vinnie knew better. Putting blinders on was how he and his mother ended up with a pregnant Gabriella at fifteen. From then on, he'd made sure his sisters were safe and let his mom have the comfort of believing her daughters were—mostly—angels.

The door opened and Stratford walked out, not quite tottering but not quite steady on his feet, either. His skin, pale as milk, stretched taut over his thin face, a faint crease in his forehead telling of pain still felt. The new bandage was much smaller than his duct tape job. Stratford managed to give Vinnie a weak smile, though, and Vinnie popped up and met him. Maybe it was his upbringing, but Vinnie wanted nothing more than to take Stratford home and feed him. Well, not *just* feed him, but definitely feed him *first*.

"Hey there. Let's get you home."

Stratford's nod was a relief. He'd been concerned Stratford was going to object again. Not that it would have mattered. Vinnie was a master at getting his own way, but he wouldn't have wanted to argue before they really got to know each other.

Normally, Vinnie would have wrapped an arm around the injured person as he guided them to the car, but without the rush of adrenaline governing their actions, he wasn't sure how well such a gesture would be received. He made sure to walk close, ready to catch Stratford if he wobbled.

By the time they'd made it back to Vinnie's parking spot, he was just about ready to sling Stratford over his shoulder and carry him, but there was an admirable determination in every step that he'd make it on his own two feet.

Vinnie clicked his automatic door release and the lights on his Navigator flashed. The sight of his car brought some energy back into Stratford's face.

"Holy overcompensation, Batman. Who needs a car this big?"

Vinnie chuckled, even as his cheeks heated at the implication his car was a substitute for his dick. With any luck, Stratford would soon learn the truth. Since the only things Vinnie could think of to say were a little too crude when he was trying to make a good impression, he kept quiet and opened the passenger door.

Stratford let out a little strangled squeak and looked at him. "I'm sorry. I didn't mean that."

"It's okay." The last thing he wanted was for Stratford to censor himself around him, but that might be too strong a sentiment to express after only a couple hours acquaintance. He wanted to get to know Stratford, and he liked the spiky sense of humor he kept glimpsing.

Stratford struggled a bit to get into the vehicle, and despite the pert little ass waving in his face, Vinnie manfully resisted the urge to grab it under the guise of helping and instead cupped Stratford's elbow to steady him.

Did they give out sainthoods to guys who didn't take the opportunity to cop a feel in a situation like this? He kind of thought he deserved one. Hell, he hadn't even taken advantage of getting Stratford's wallet out of his back pocket earlier. He got Stratford settled and helped him do up his seatbelt because that hand wasn't up to much movement. Covertly, he let his fingers linger on Stratford's body—nowhere sexual—as long as he could without seeming like a total pervert.

Within seconds, he'd rounded the car, opened his door, and bounded into his seat. "We should be okay parking on the street outside the community center for a few minutes. Let them know you're okay."

Stratford winced. "Do I, uh, have to go in with you?"

A smile fought its way to Vinnie's lips, but he did his best to suppress it. Shouldn't be anything embarrassing about getting hurt, but his sisters were the same. "No, of course not. It will only be a minute or two, and I can run in by myself. Just so they don't worry."

Stratford wouldn't meet his eyes, so a change of subject was in order.

"Did they give you a prescription? We can get it filled before I drop you at home."

"They gave me some pills. No prescription. They said after these were gone, regular pain killers would do."

"Okay, then, what's your address?"

As Stratford spoke, Vinnie typed it into the GPS on the dash. When the route lit up, he bit back a groan. As much as Stratford probably just wanted to crash in his own bed, Vinnie had been hoping the drive would be longer than a few blocks. Nevertheless, he put the car into gear and headed for Stratford's place.

"What's the prognosis?"

Stratford sighed. "Four stitches. Probably no nerve or tendon damage, but they warned me if I have issues to come back in. They did tell me to rest it, but I work on a computer all day. I don't know how much I can rest it."

"So take a few sick days. Surely your boss wouldn't want you to permanently injure yourself over this."

A one-shouldered shrug was his only response. The stirrings of anger kindled in his belly. What kind of employer did Stratford have, that he'd be so concerned about taking sick days?

"Please, promise me. Take at least one day off. Give yourself a break."

Vinnie pulled into a parking lot at his GPS's direction. Too soon. "You live above a medical clinic?" It wasn't an urgent care and was already long closed, but the irony was not lost on him.

"Yeah, kind of. I think they mostly specialize in weight loss, though."

Stratford fumbled at the door handle.

"I'll get it, hold on. You should probably start resting that hand right now." Vinnie exited the car and rounded it to open Stratford's door, helping him down.

With an awkward movement, Stratford pulled his keys out of his right-hand jacket pocket.

"Thank you for everything."

"Did you want me to walk you up?" *Or stay with you the night?* As much as Vinnie wanted to learn everything about Stratford, from what he did for a living to what he looked like when coming his brains out, Vinnie was 100 percent certain that staying the night tonight—even just to take care of Stratford—wasn't in the cards.

A tiny frown creased Stratford's forehead. "No, thank you, I'm fine. How did you get to be so good in a crisis?"

"Oh, kids. They're always breaking bones or getting hurt. I've practically got frequent flyer miles at my local urgent care."

Stratford's eyes narrowed. "Yes, of course. Thank you for helping me. I have to go now."

Stunned, Vinnie watched as Stratford unlocked the door and practically ran up a steep flight of steps. His feet were out of view by the time the door swung shut behind him.

Why had Stratford spooked like that? And why hadn't Vinnie even asked for his phone number? Knowing Stratford's name and address, he could easily get it, but he'd have to think about whether that would be stalker-like. Wanting into Stratford's pants, combined with his inexperience at dating, had thrown his judgment all out of whack.

Three

STRATFORD considered the stairs. It had been a week since his disastrous date with Barry, but now, he wasn't so sure it qualified as one of his worst ones. Certainly not as bad as the fiasco of cooking class on Tuesday. He should have listened to Abby. Cooking was a skill beyond him, as was acting like a normal human being.

Fuck it. He was taking the elevator, even if it meant he might run into Barry. It wouldn't be any more humiliating than running into Vinnie. He'd made a complete ass of himself in front of Vinnie, and then, at the end of the shittastic night, he found out Vinnie had kids. Which meant Vinnie was a super-nice guy, completely off limits to the gay moron he'd ended up partnered with, and Stratford was out a hundred and fifty bucks for half of one cooking class. The only thing he'd learned was that he was never going to devein a shrimp. Considering his cooking skills, it was a sure bet he'd never need that knowledge anyway.

Flexing his hand, he strode to the elevators, head held high, and stabbed the up button. The wait was excruciating as he surreptitiously inspected each new arrival for Barry.

The elevator doors dinged, and Stratford sighed with relief as he got inside. His natural avoidance mechanism probably was every bit as childish as Abby told him it was, but ever since the shock of his parents disowning him, he had a hard time facing situations where he might be rejected. By rights he shouldn't have dated at all, but the search for a boyfriend was the one romanticized hope that could overcome his fear of rejection. Of course, it usually meant he did weird shit like running from exes or past fucks or uncomfortable situations. Or rejecting people before they got the chance to do it.

Like Barry. He'd done the rejecting... or at least, it was implied when he'd told Barry he was going to the bar for a drink and had continued right out the door of the club.

At least it would be easier to avoid Vinnie.

The elevator disgorged a few people on Barry's floor, and Stratford sucked in a breath. He forced himself to stand tall and face forward. So what if Barry saw him as the doors shut?

But he was spared that, at least.

Seconds later, he'd opened the glass door leading to the Nectar offices. The receptionist, who, thanks to Stratford's cursed job would be forever labeled Trey the Twink in his mind, waved him over.

"Hey, Trey." As he did every time he spoke to Trey, Stratford had to bite back "the Twink" from his greeting. "What's up?"

"I hope you're feeling better." Trey pouted, and Stratford frowned. Was Trey giving him fake sympathy because... no, he didn't know why Trey would be sympathetic at all. Just because they were both gay didn't mean they had to like each other, and since Trey never, ever seemed genuine, Stratford had written him off as a lost cause. But as the office administrative assistant, Stratford didn't have a choice about ignoring him completely. If he wanted his invoices paid or supplies to arrive in a timely manner, he had to be polite.

"Thanks. I'm hoping it won't get too much in the way." Stratford held up his bandaged hand.

Trey the Twink snickered. "Wow. I didn't even know it was possible to choke the chicken enough to damage yourself."

Preventing the eye roll was actually painful. Ever since he'd been saddled with the pen name Doctor Chicken, everyone at the Nectar offices had made some sort of reference to masturbating with that exact same euphemism—out of Gonzalez's hearing, of course. But he'd been Doctor Chicken for over four years now, and most of Nectar's employees had gotten their juvenile licks in ages ago. Trey was very young and still fairly new to Nectar. Stratford's mood sank as he

35

realized he might have become Doctor Chicken while Trey the Twink was still in high school.

"Ha-ha. I cut myself cooking."

Trey's eyes widened, and he giggled some more. Stratford didn't give a shit what Trey the Twink found so funny about him cooking. It wasn't as though Trey had ever seen his place and knew about his dismal kitchen situation.

He gestured with his thumb over his shoulder. "Okay, then, I'm going to get to work."

Instead, Trey reached out, faster than a striking snake, and grabbed his arm, almost making him drop his latte and the white chocolate scone he'd bought as a treat. "Wait a moment."

Stratford halted, but Trey's intensity and weird expression were making him nervous. Was he in trouble for taking a sick day? At least he had stitches to prove why he'd taken Wednesday off.

"I'm really sorry your date with Barry didn't work out." Trey's lips twisted, and Stratford realized the weird expression on his face was sympathy, or the closest facsimile Trey could manage.

"Uh, thanks." What else did he say? Barry the Biter must have told Trey about it. Stratford swallowed. How on earth had Barry spun that story? Maybe he'd have to suck it up and face Barry. Find out what he was saying. Tell him to shut his mouth. Nicely, though. Barry could probably break him like a twig if he was of a mind to.

"Yeah, so I was hoping you won't be mad if I start dating him. We're going out tonight. I would have mentioned it yesterday, but you were sick." Trey did an absolute shit job of hiding the triumphant glee under his fake sympathy.

"Uh, no. I won't be mad." Assuming a person wanted to prance through the minefield that was dating a friend's ex, asking permission was only polite. He and Trey weren't friends, though, which meant Trey had another reason for telling him. Because Stratford hadn't missed that Trey hadn't phrased it in the form of a question.

"Oh, I'm so glad. It's probably better this way." Trey patted his arm. "Not everyone can handle passionate, kinky sex."

Stratford raised his brows. So that's how Barry the Biter was selling it. Stratford was a prudish, vanilla loser. Awesome.

Trey wasn't done. "I'm not surprised he scared you. Sex clubs can be a little terrifying the first time." Trey gasped and held his hands to his chest like a Southern belle about to have the vapors. "You aren't a virgin, are you?"

This time, Stratford let the eye roll escape as he turned toward his desk, the sound of Trey's spiteful laughter floating along behind him. He certainly wasn't going to stand at the reception desk and stamp his feet claiming he wasn't a virgin. That would be beyond pathetic. How dare Barry—and Trey—imply that he was scared of sex. Trey was practically a neonate and acted like they were in grade school. Stratford was twenty-nine—he wasn't going to lower himself to their level. Judging by Barry's actions, apparently Stratford should have sent out an interoffice memo about Barry's sad lack of skills in the blowjob department. He hoped Trey had a Teflon willie, because he was going to need it.

His job sucked. His life sucked. And he couldn't even get his dick sucked properly.

STRATFORD dropped into his chair and set his latte down to the right of his computer. It was only nine, and he wanted to be… not here. He would have called in sick again, but he couldn't bear to stay at home another day. If his hand had been up to doing some sketching, that would have been a different story. But the only thing he could do was hang out in his tiny apartment and watch television in between popping out for multiple lattes during the day. The best thing about hanging out at his apartment was his collection of geek-friendly DVDs and cuddling with Bob. A fifteen-pound purr machine was an excellent cure for depression.

Unfortunately, after spending the entire previous weekend having a *Doctor Who* marathon, he was out of patience for hanging around his apartment. The job at Nectar might be complete shit, but at least it gave him something to think about besides how shitty the rest of his life was.

"Hey there, chicken boy. Heard you couldn't put out." Derek the Dweeb passed his desk and snickered.

Derek didn't like gay people. Or so it seemed. However, he did seem to have an unnatural interest in Stratford's sex life, especially since he'd seen fit to discuss it with either Trey or Barry. Idiot.

He wondered, briefly, why Barry had waited a week to start carrying tales to his coworkers, but found he didn't care. Like everything else, it would go away if he just ignored it.

The noise of his computer powering up covered the sound of any footsteps, and when a hand landed on his shoulder, he jumped.

"Glad you're here." Stratford spun his desk chair around to face his boss.

"Thanks." Amazing. Mr. Gonzalez had never cared about his welfare before. Only the bottom line. Maybe he'd been too cynical about his work.

"You're heading into crunch time on this new project." Mr. Gonzalez slapped a fat blue file folder down on his desk.

Right. Stupid of him to think his welfare would matter to anyone here. He hated this damned job. Three more years. That was all.

"I'll take a look at it."

"Good." Gonzalez walked away through the cube farm, heading for his office.

Hopefully the new project wouldn't require much in the way of sketching. He'd just turned in the sketches for *Doctor Chicken Grows Bubble Bushes* ahead of schedule. He had another week or so before he had to hand in the storyboards for *Doctor Chicken and the Snotty Squirrels*, but he could pop those out in an afternoon. Gonzalez always had tons of revisions, whether he spent twelve hours or twelve days putting it together. The man worshipped his red marker and probably got the shakes if he didn't get to use it.

The galleys were done for *Doctor Chicken's Fish Fables*, and he'd been planning to work on a new line of Doctor Chicken greeting cards because he could just repurpose images from recent books and come up with some pithy, rhyming captions.

After shoving the folder to the edge of his desk, he began his morning setup. There were certain programs he liked to have open and at the tip of his fingers at all times, even if it meant there were a number of applications and windows open at any given time.

"What did you do, honey?" Paula leaned over his monitor and grabbed his hand. The office "mother," Paula, was in charge of the sickly sweet inspirational cards with pictures of flowers. She was the only one who hadn't made snide remarks about choking the chicken. Probably because she was too sweet and matronly to even know what that meant.

If he could have done it all over again, he'd have come up with something else besides Doctor Chicken. He'd been sure it was going to give him the leverage to make a name for himself or get him experience he could use to springboard his true goal—graphic novels—while giving him a regular paycheck. By the time management had bought into the idea and given the go-ahead, he was already regretting the stupid name he'd chosen. Not long after, he'd realized he'd sold himself into Doctor Chicken slavery. Once the idea had taken off, he'd been pulled off all other projects, and he'd been stuck in full-time chicken hell ever since.

"Cut myself at cooking class."

"Cooking class? That's a great idea, honey. You've got a better chance of meeting a nice boy there than going out with that punk Barry."

The amusement of hearing Paula call anyone, much less clean-cut Barry, a punk was enough to partially offset the embarrassment that simply everyone knew about his failed date with Barry and undoubtedly thought he couldn't handle sex.

"Uh, yeah. I guess."

"Young people nowadays don't realize that sex is so much better when there's some emotion to go with it, a decent relationship."

"Uh-huh." He did not want to discuss sex with Paula. Not at all.

"You're a good guy, Stratford. You'll find your knight in shining armor."

Knight in shining armor? He wasn't some helpless damsel, for God's sake. He didn't need someone to save him. He'd been on his own since he was nineteen. Abby had been his knight that first year after his parents disowned him, but every goddamned thing he'd done or had since had been the result of his own hard work. If it had been anyone else telling him he'd find a knight, he'd tell them to go to hell, but he couldn't do that with Paula. Not when he knew she only meant it in the best possible way.

"Thanks, Paula. But I better see what I missed yesterday."

"Okay, honey, but let me know if you need anything." Paula continued on to the copier.

Resolutely ignoring the folder that undoubtedly held some fresh chicken torture dreamed up by Nectar's marketing whiz kids, Stratford opened the inbox with his, or rather, Doctor Chicken's, fan mail. Doctor Chicken was designed for the four-to-six-year age group, and he didn't really think kids that age were as erudite as some of the letters led him to believe, but he didn't know shit all about kids. He had no idea if the kids typed out e-mails to him themselves or if they dictated to mom or dad, but either way, he got a surprising amount of pleasure out of getting fan mail. He had a store of Doctor Chicken–themed e-mail templates, and he only ever needed to send a few simple lines to make them happy.

A couple hours later, with both his and his alter ego's inboxes dealt with, Stratford grimaced and pulled the blue folder toward him.

A minute later his stomach dropped into his socks and sweat broke out on his upper lip. He grabbed the folder and dashed off to Gonzalez's office.

"Mr. Gonzalez. I was just looking over this folder. You can't seriously expect me to start making personal appearances."

He couldn't. Just couldn't. Speaking in public ranked up there with ripping out his toenails. Never mind that little fact about him knowing nothing about kids.

"Of course we can. It's in your contract. We decided some extra publicity is a good thing. We can sweep up for Christmas gifts, then use it to boost the January slump, since the new online game had to be postponed until February. The libraries are gagging for you to do some reading circles or such crap. Just make sure when you set up your schedule that you put the majority of your appearances in Nectar stores. Don't want those greasy little rug rats to escape with too many freebies. No sense hiring an actor when you're easy enough on the eyes."

Stratford's stomach flipped. He may not know anything about kids, but he certainly didn't have the contempt for them that his bosses did. "I have to set up my own schedule?"

"Yes. Well, except for this Saturday. Marketing set up a gig at the flagship store at the big mall, getting in the week before Black Friday and before old goat Santa gets in there. They've done all the advertising, so you can use their plan to get started with the rest of the appearances. You'll probably need to do a few on the weekends, so we'll work out some flex time. I'd like to see two appearances, within driving distance, per week, but minimum of one per week until launch."

Gonzalez tapped a pen against his lips for a moment before he spoke. "You can skip Thanksgiving week. We'd get lost in the confusion, but I still want to see a preliminary schedule by Monday, end of day."

He hadn't even gotten to the marketing plan part of the folder before he'd stormed into Gonzalez's office. "Uh, I don't have a car." Stratford's voice shook. Saturday? He had to work Saturday and read to little kids. Gonzalez had magnanimously given him Thanksgiving weekend off, which was a relief, if only because he couldn't imagine trying to book space anywhere in the post-Black Friday chaos.

"Do you have a license?"

"Yes."

"Well, then, rent one."

Because, of course, Stratford's personal budget ran to renting cars willy-nilly. His boss was a fucking ass.

Gonzalez's phone rang. "The information's all in the folder. I have to take this." He shooed Stratford away.

Stratford's heartbeat sped up, and he started breathing rapidly. By the time he got back to his desk, he was lightheaded and his vision was graying at the edges. He slumped down in his chair, folder falling from nerveless fingers.

"Honey, honey, slow down. Deep breaths in and out." Like magic, Paula was there in front of him, hands warm on his shoulders. "You're hyperventilating."

Stratford forced himself to follow Paula's directions. Slowly, his breathing and heart rate returned to normal.

"What's the matter? You shot out of your chair like your butt was on fire."

"I have to do some public readings as Doctor Chicken."

"Oh, the kids will love that. What a great idea."

Paula would think it was a good idea. She patted him on the cheek. "Don't you worry. No baby talk, and most kids want to tell you stuff without any prompting. Just let them, and smile and pay attention. Don't condescend to them, because they'll know. But they're going to love you. Maybe you should take an early lunch. Take two hours, get your head on straight. I'll cover for you."

"Thanks, Paula." He might just do that.

She stood and ruffled his hair like he was a kid himself before heading back to her own desk.

He was almost afraid to tell Abby about this latest development. She would tell him what she always did when he complained about his job—find a new one. She thought Nectar was taking advantage of him, and while he could admit she was right, the thought of going through the uncertainty of a new job when he was skating on the edge of bankruptcy scared the ever-loving shit out of him. He'd been working for Nectar since he got out of college, and while the pay wasn't great, he'd gotten regular raises. Would he even be able to get the same amount of money somewhere else? He should have taken a course to brush up on his skills instead of signing up for a cooking course he'd never use because he'd wanted a straight man he could never have and would never see again.

This new project at least gave him a legitimate reason to work late tonight instead of sitting at home wondering if that blond bimbo had managed to get her hooks into Vinnie at cooking class. If he took an alternate route home, he'd be able to walk right past the community center, take another peek inside the window. That couldn't hurt.

"HEY, mama, just stopped by to say hello." Going home in between work and evening plans was rare. Usually Vinnie just worked late and got home around eight or nine, in time to sit down to a late dinner. But since his schedule had recently eased up, Vinnie had time for plans in the evening. After fifteen years of acting as head of the household, he appreciated the chance to get out and do something besides work and act as a parent to his sisters. With his mom, three mostly grown sisters and one young niece, the family home was busting at the seams.

"Aren't you going to stay for dinner?"

Vinnie kissed his mom's cheek. The warm, familiar scents of tomato sauce and fresh basil made his stomach grumble in protest. It was very much conditioned to expect feeding when his mom made the kitchen smell so good.

"Nope. I've got my cooking class tonight. But save me something I can warm up, just in case." Last time, the leftovers had come in handy when he'd returned after dropping Stratford at home.

"Oh, yes, your cooking class. How is that poor boy doing?"

Vinnie blushed, something he rarely did. "I don't know. And he's not a boy." Thank God.

His mother tsked. "You didn't even call to see how he was doing? That's not like you."

"I didn't… get his number." Vinnie checked the fridge for a bottle of water, letting the cool air chill his cheeks so his blush didn't get even more noticeable.

"Oh, I see." His mother's tone was knowing and hopeful at the same time.

"You see what, mama?" Evie skidded into the kitchen with the boundless energy of a teenager. She might be his sister, but more so than his other sisters, he was protective of her. Evie was the only one of them with no real memory of their father, and it wasn't beyond the bounds of possibility that Vinnie could have fathered a seventeen-year-old. Hell, Sienna's father had been only sixteen, and Gabriella fifteen, when she'd been conceived. But Evie might be the closest he'd have to a child of his own. Unfortunately, the teen years were taking their toll, and she'd yet to grow out of her dramatic yet petulant and occasionally sullen phase. He didn't remember Marissa or Gabriella being quite so willful, but then, he worked such long hours to get his business going, he might have been too tired to notice.

"Your brother met someone."

"Mama!" How did she know? And why had she felt the need to announce it? "It's nothing."

Evie gave him a look wise beyond her years. "Whatever, Vinnie. Hey, does this mean I can go out with Mario?"

"No. Mario is too old for you." Their mother was adamant.

Vinnie wasn't so sure, but Evie was only seventeen and prone to distraction. Vinnie had made a point to meet Mario, because he'd been leery of a twenty-one-year-old wanting to date his seventeen-year-old sister. The kid had seemed nice enough, and his mom went to church with Mario's mom, but he was willing to accept his mother's decision on this, and Evie should be too.

"Vinnie! It's not fair. If I don't date him, Shelby will!"

Vinnie clenched his teeth together. "Listen to your mama, Evie. And life isn't fair. You should be concentrating on your schoolwork, otherwise you'll never get into college." He might have to drop by the church sometime, put a bug in Mrs. Pontarelli's ear about the whole impending romance. God knew, his mother would never do it.

"College, college, college. That's all you ever talk about! What if I want to go backpacking in Europe or go to Hollywood to become an actress?"

Vinnie opened his water and gulped some down. This was a familiar argument. "Then you can do it after you graduate college and have a job to support yourself while you do it."

"It's not fair."

As though a curtain had dropped, Evie had turned from a sunny, vivacious person to a virago. She whirled around and stormed out of the room. "I hate you both!"

Vinnie looked at his mom and shrugged. It hadn't been the first time they'd heard that. Evie might be the most dramatic of his three sisters, but all of them had a hot Mediterranean temper.

"Ha. Mario doesn't realize we're saving him from disaster."

"Vinnie, Vinnie." His mother's tone was disapproving.

"Sorry, Mama." It was true. One day, Evie was going to need a man with some maturity on him, one that wouldn't let her chew him up and spit him out. Even with an extra four years, Mario wasn't ready to take on his sister. And for that, Vinnie was secretly glad.

"Where's Sienna?"

"Gabriella took her out to buy a new dress and eat out."

That explained why the house was as quiet as it was. Marissa was still at work. She'd turned into even more of a workaholic than he was. Then again, he'd become a workaholic out of necessity. Marissa was just wired that way. An overachiever all the way.

"Bring your man for dinner. We'd love to meet him. What's his name?"

Vinnie grimaced. He thought he'd been getting ahead of himself with his sudden fascination with Stratford. They hadn't even exchanged phone numbers; meeting the mother might be a little overwhelming. He wasn't even a hundred percent sure Stratford liked him.

Hey, Stratford. Are you gay? What's your favorite color? Oh, and yeah, my mom wants to meet you. Come over to the house for dinner.

That wouldn't be weird at all.

"I gotta go, or I'm going to be late." Yes, he was a coward. His love life might be sparse, but his sex life hadn't been, and neither of them was he going to discuss with his mother. "Give Sienna a kiss for me, I'll be home after her bedtime."

Vinnie escaped, as eager to get away from the probing questions as he was to see Stratford again. Would Stratford care that he lived at home still? He'd planned on getting his own place once Evie went to college, but it never occurred to him to think about what would happen if he wanted to bring a boyfriend home before then. Getting sex at a club wasn't hard, but now he was looking for something more. He loved his family and his work, but the time was right for him to find someone he could call his own and he already had prime candidate in Stratford. Oh, he wanted to get Stratford into bed—and soon—but he wanted to take it slow. When the time came, though, he hoped Stratford had a place of his own.

VINNIE sat in a small booth, his back to the door, sipping his mocha. Years in the shop had inured him to thick, black, tar-like coffee, but as soon as he'd gotten his business off the ground, he'd been able to afford coffees in cafés like this one, and had soon discovered that coffee could taste good, rather than just a means to a temporary jolt to wakefulness.

The walls were covered with the works of local artists, on sale by consignment. Some of them good, some of them bad, but all contributing to make the little independent cafe seem a bit bohemian, a bit art house, and far removed from the chains. He had to give Stratford credit, because not only was the atmosphere good, the mocha was excellent—best he'd had in some time.

Sighing, he checked his watch. Coming to Stratford's favorite coffee house after cooking class was a stupid idea. The disappointment at Stratford's absence from the class had been almost overwhelming. He was also worried. What if something had gone wrong with his hand? He'd been completely distracted the whole class; he was lucky he hadn't ended up at the urgent care clinic with an injury of his own. Every time someone walked in the room, he'd looked up, hoping Stratford was just late. But no such luck. The minutes ticked by, and with each one that passed, Vinnie lost any hope of seeing Stratford. Hell, he'd even whirled around a few times and peered out the window, the sensation of someone watching him crawling up his back.

He wanted nothing more than to go and knock on Stratford's door, but he wasn't even sure if the door he'd seen would lead up to a single apartment or twelve. If it was more than one apartment, it was a little late—and a little weird—to knock on each one looking for a guy he'd spent a few hours with. He'd probably get himself arrested or a seventy-two-hour psych lockup.

None of that changed the fact that he was worried. He could admit to himself that worry wasn't the only reason. He'd intended to ask Stratford on a date, but as he accepted that Stratford hadn't come to class, he'd also seen dreams crumble, dreams he had no right basing on a guy he barely knew.

That hadn't stopped him from heading straight for this cafe the minute the class ended. He'd scanned the patrons, desperately searching for the tousled head of brown hair and wide brown eyes that he had no trouble picturing late at night in bed.

Again he was destined to be disappointed. He had chosen a table based on the fact that it faced the cash register. If, by chance, Stratford came in for a coffee, he didn't want to miss it. As soon as he finished his coffee, he'd have to decide if he was going to make a fool of himself at Stratford's apartment, checking up on him. Hell, for all

Vinnie knew, the man had gone home to let his mom baby him. Or maybe the man had a boyfriend or girlfriend who was taking care of him.

If Vinnie came off as a freaky stalker, then Stratford would never come back to class.

Staring down into the dregs of his mocha, now nothing more than a mouthful of chocolate syrup, he still hadn't made a decision. With another heavy sigh, he downed the last swallow, and almost choked on it when he noticed who was standing at the counter. He didn't know how Stratford had managed to enter the cafe without him noticing, but he wasn't letting the guy leave without at least finding out how his hand was.

Vinnie wiped frantically at his lips, not wanting to be wearing a mocha mustache when Stratford turned around. Stratford stripped off a pair of cheap stretchy knit gloves that barely contained his long fingers and palms and stuffed them in a pocket of the same thin jacket he'd been wearing on Tuesday. Narrow shoulders shivering, Stratford blew on his hands to warm them while waiting for the barista to fill his order.

The girl behind the counter clearly knew him. "We've got some of those cinnamon buns you like."

Stratford groaned. "I really shouldn't."

The girl waited with an expectant expression, and Stratford caved.

"Okay, okay." He continued to rub his hands together.

Where had Stratford been that he'd gotten so chilled? With his sparse frame, he should also be wearing a thicker coat and better gloves. The cold November winds promised a long, bitter winter. The man was heading toward pneumonia.

As soon as Stratford was handed his cup and a bag with his pastry, Vinnie stood so he'd be in front of Stratford when he turned.

When Stratford faced him, it took him a minute to register Vinnie as someone other than an obstacle on his way to the door.

"Hello."

Stratford's eyes widened, and for a brief moment, Vinnie saw pleasure in that thin pale face. Then pink spots bloomed on his sharp cheekbones, matching the ruddy windburn on his forehead and chin, and his eyes darted around as though searching for a place to hide.

"I have a table over here." Vinnie waved a hand at his booth. "Why don't you come join me? Warm up for a bit before you head out into the cold again?"

"Uh, sure."

Vinnie sat in the same seat he'd been in. Stratford sat across from him, butt perched on the edge of his seat as though he was going to tear ass out the door the second Vinnie glanced away. Tuesday night he'd managed to smooth away some of Stratford's skittishness, and he hoped he could do it again. If he couldn't, this attraction was going to crash and burn, because Stratford would never let him in.

"How's your hand?"

Stratford held it up and tilted his palm back and forth. "Okay. Sore still, but I was able to work today."

"Good. I'm glad. Missed you in class today."

The pink on his cheeks darkened to red. "Oh, well, I wasn't very good at it, was I? With the cut, I figured I'd be even worse."

Vinnie shrugged. "I would have been happy to do the work if you'd kept me company."

"Actually, I was thinking of finding out if I could get a refund."

Disappointment welled up in Vinnie's chest, hot and bitter.

"If you quit, how are you going to save me from Bethany?" Vinnie had been lucky enough to pair up with a college professor whose husband hadn't been able to come to the class because of a conference, but next class he was fair game, and Bethany had him in her sights. Of course, that wasn't the only reason he didn't want Stratford to quit.

Although Stratford's blush didn't abate, he relaxed a fraction into his seat. "Oh. Yeah, she likes you, doesn't she? She's pretty, but your wife's got to be hot."

Vinnie bit back a groan. There was no mistaking the unadulterated admiration in Stratford's eyes. He was taking this man on a date. No doubt about it.

"No wife, no girlfriend." His voice had dropped to an unexpectedly seductive timbre.

His words weren't enough to erase Stratford's puzzled look. "So why didn't you want to work with…." The shoe dropped and Stratford's eyes widened as he stared at Vinnie.

"But what about your kids?" Stratford's voice had suddenly become suspicious, almost accusing.

Kids? "I don't have any kids."

Stratford frowned. "When we were at the clinic, you said you were good in a crisis because of your kids."

Vinnie's confusion cleared. "Oh, no. Not my kids. My sisters are a lot younger than I am. When they got hurt I was the one who ended up taking them to the emergency room."

"Oh. I see." Stratford seemed even more relaxed after the explanation.

Taking a chance, Vinnie stretched out a hand and covered one of Stratford's still-chilled ones. "Would you go out to dinner with me tomorrow night?" There'd be plenty of time, then, to share the specifics of his home life while he found out about Stratford's.

"Tomorrow? Friday night?"

Disappointment surged again. "If you don't have plans. Or, uh, a boyfriend who'd be upset." Oh, shit. He'd forgot to ask if Stratford had a boyfriend. *Please don't let him have a boyfriend.*

"Oh, no. No plans, no boyfriend." Stratford glanced down at Vinnie's hand where it lay over his, then back up into Vinnie's eyes. "Are you sure?"

Letting his thumb stroke gently against Stratford's skin, Vinnie tried to project his sincerity as best he could. "Absolutely."

"Um. Okay, sure."

"I'll pick you up at seven?"

"Seven. Sure."

"Can I get your number, just in case I end up running late?" Vinnie had no intention of running late, but he wanted Stratford's number.

They exchanged numbers with a minimum of fuss. He was tempted to stay and get to know more about Stratford now, but he'd rather tease information out of the man in a much more romantic setting than this one, however comfortable it was.

"I have an early meeting, so I need to get going. Did you want a lift home?"

Stratford's gaze dropped, and Vinnie couldn't tell what he was thinking.

"No, it's not far to walk. I'll finish my coffee here."

He'd prefer to make sure Stratford got home safely, but he was a grown man, and Vinnie had to respect his wishes. He didn't want to do anything to make Stratford reconsider their date. "Okay then. I'll see you tomorrow at seven."

"Seven. Perfect."

Four

VINNIE pulled into the parking lot at Stratford's apartment on the dot of seven, more nervous than he'd been in a long time. He parked in the same spot as when he'd dropped Stratford off the other night, got out of the car, and smoothed down the edges of his leather jacket. The clinic on the first floor was long closed, and the parking lot was empty. Gazing up at the small building, he counted windows. If the entire upper floor was apartments, there probably weren't more than four.

With a frown he peered around. He hadn't taken note of it before, but there wasn't a lot of lighting around the building, considering this was the home of at least one person.

He walked up to the door and rattled the handle. At least it was locked—one less thing to worry about. Peering in the dark, he couldn't find a doorbell or a buzzer or anything. Stepping back, he pulled out his phone and called Stratford.

It rang several times before Stratford picked up.

"Hello? Vinnie? Is something wrong?"

Vinnie shivered a little at the sound of Stratford's voice despite the hesitation.

"Hey. I'm downstairs, but I don't see a buzzer."

"Oh. I guess the ivy's covered it up again. I'll be down in a minute."

Vinnie tried to peer at the wall again, but between the shadows and the ivy, he had no idea where the buzzer might be hidden. Instead he stood by the grill of his car and waited. He'd have rather been invited up so he could see where Stratford lived, but there would be plenty of opportunity for that, he hoped.

The door swung open and Stratford stepped out. Vinnie shook his head. If he and Stratford managed to see Christmas together, he was going to buy Stratford a decent pair of gloves. The edge of a bow tie peeking out above the collar made him smile. He'd been surprised at how much he loved the bow tie look and was glad it seemed to be a regular part of Stratford's wardrobe.

The wind whipped the edge of Stratford's jacket up, and Vinnie realized it was the thin bit of nothing he'd been wearing at the coffee shop. If Vinnie didn't see evidence of a proper winter coat soon, Stratford would be getting one of those too. Before Christmas.

"Hi." Stratford gave him a little smile, looking into his eyes. Very little of his skittishness was apparent, which was good. Vinnie didn't mind soothing Stratford's ruffles, but he'd hoped the more Stratford got to know him, the less flustered he'd get.

"Hey." Vinnie smiled back, content to stand there staring. When Stratford crossed his arms over his chest and tucked his hands into his pits, Vinnie shook himself. "We've got reservations at seven thirty, so we'd better get going."

Taking a few steps back, he opened the passenger door for Stratford and moved far enough back to let Stratford in. Again, he was tempted to grab Stratford's ass as the guy hoisted himself into the Navigator, but he refrained. Vinnie had done a lot more intimate things with guys at clubs, and he never even knew their names, but he was hoping for something more than a quick bang in a back alley with Stratford.

As soon as he got the car started and back out on the road, Vinnie turned up the heat a bit higher than he normally had it because he was almost certain Stratford felt the cold more than he did. He also stretched a hand out to turn on the seat warmer for the passenger side.

For a few minutes, unsure what to say, they sat in uncomfortable silence. Then Stratford squeaked and shifted in his seat.

"What the hell?"

Vinnie took his eyes off the road to glance over at Stratford's horrified expression, directed toward his lap.

"Oh, I'm sorry. I thought you'd like the seat warmer. Is it too hot for you?"

Laughter sputtered out of Stratford. "No, no, it's good. I just thought for a minute I'd lost control of my bladder and pissed myself."

Vinnie laughed too. "Well, I guess I'm glad you didn't."

"Not as glad as I am! I like this feature, though. I don't have a car, and my friend Abby, her car's a piece of shit, so no nice seat warmers in there."

"I have to admit, I kind of spoiled myself with the car. The seats will also cool down in the summer."

"Fuck, really? Air-conditioned seats? That's amazing."

"I like it."

"Yeah, nothing worse than overheating your junk on sun-warmed leather."

Vinnie nodded, but was too distracted by the mention of Stratford's dick to think of a coherent way to continue the conversation.

Stratford seemed content to fiddle with his radio stations, so the rest of the drive to the restaurant was spent in comfortable silence broken only by the strains of some nineties alt rock.

Traffic worked in their favor, and Vinnie pulled into the tiny parking lot at twenty after seven. Even with a fairly early reservation—for a Friday—the parking lot was full.

"*Bos*? This is where we're going?"

"Yeah. Oh, shit. Are you a vegetarian?" Mentally, Vinnie kicked himself for not asking before making reservations at one of the best steakhouses in the city. He was really shit at this dating stuff. And his mind was a complete blank about someplace decent they could go last minute on a Friday night.

"Oh, no, it's just... am I dressed okay? It's kinda upscale, isn't it?"

"You're dressed fine." As long as Stratford wasn't wearing a T-shirt or a mesh shirt with his bow tie. Vinnie wanted to make a good impression, and he hoped he had. "It's a little upscale, sure, but it still feels really relaxed inside."

"Okay, then. I've heard great things about this place."

"You up to walking a couple of blocks, or should I just get valet parking?" Vinnie didn't normally bother with valet parking, and the wind had died down a bit. Walking a bit after dinner, taking in the neighborhood Christmas lights, which had just recently gone up, maybe holding hands, sounded like an ideal after-dinner activity. There was even a movie theatre a couple of blocks away. Dinner and a movie might be a complete cliché, but maybe there was a reason it was cliché. It made a solid first date.

"I'm okay walking."

"You won't be too cold?" Vinnie pinched the sleeve of Stratford's jacket and rubbed the fabric between his fingers.

"Nah. I'm fine."

Vinnie maneuvered the big vehicle around and pulled out of the parking lot, heading for the larger public lot over on the next street. Selfishly, he decided if Stratford got too cold he could always wrap an arm around him, as he'd done when he'd walked them to the urgent care facility.

Traffic and pedestrians weren't nearly as favorable for the short stretch of road he had to traverse, and they ended up almost speed walking back to the restaurant, arriving five minutes later than their reservation.

ONCE they were seated, Vinnie tucked his nose in the menu, covertly observing Stratford's reaction over the large black folder.

"I wonder why they called it *Bos*." Stratford hadn't even opened his menu yet, too busy checking out the ambiance.

"I asked the same thing when I was here last. Apparently it's the genus name for cattle, *Bos taurus*. I think it's the species name for beef cattle. Something like that."

It was times like this when Vinnie felt stupid. He may have created a successful business out of almost nothing, but he still was only high school educated. He read tons of articles and nonfiction books, when he had the time, but talking Latin names for species was a little out of his depth.

"Interesting. Far classier than just calling it *Cattle* or *Find Meat Here* or something."

Vinnie smirked. Funny and fiery. Somehow he'd just known, and he wanted to see more of it.

Stratford bit his lip and glanced down at his lap before speaking again. "So, you've been here before, have you?"

"Once. I was meeting a couple of lawyers about some contracts." He'd been surprised by the casual atmosphere, but he'd also found it far more romantic than necessary. Didn't make dealing with contracts any more appealing, either. At least he now had Marissa to work on his contracts. Just having someone else work on the evil things was worth every penny he spent toward her MBA. "Despite the fact they told me it was one of their business expenses, I'm pretty sure I footed the bill for it, considering the invoice they sent me."

"Oh. Seems like an odd place for a business meeting."

"Yep. I think they were just looking for an excuse to eat here. Mind you, once I'd tried the steak, I could hardly blame them."

He'd been waiting for the perfect occasion to make a return trip, and as soon as he'd decided to ask Stratford out, this was the first place that had come to mind. He gazed into Stratford's eyes for long moments, but when his heart rate accelerated and his dick began to thicken, he glanced back down at his menu. Screwing up the first date by making it all about sex would guarantee he wouldn't have a second date… at least, not one that led to a relationship. Sex he was good at; relationships he needed to tread a little more carefully.

"Do you drink wine? I could order a bottle." Would a tipsy Stratford be more or less clumsy?

"I like it well enough, but I don't know anything about it."

"Neither do I. I usually have a bottle or two of Chianti at the house, but I always buy the same brand. I can't decide if I should take a course in that as well." Wine snobbery was another subject on which he keenly felt the lack of a college education. Not that college taught anything more than extracurricular beer appreciation, based on what he'd seen of his sisters' college experiences, but the lack of knowledge reminded him that those same wine snobs would likely look down on him—whatever his successes had been—if they knew he only had a high-school education.

Stratford flashed him a relieved smile. "Me too. Except I probably wouldn't be able to afford whatever wines I learned about anyway, so I've put a pin in that for later. Not that I want to become one of those wine snobs."

"No, I know what you mean. I'd just like to learn enough to understand a bit about what I was ordering."

Raising an eyebrow, Stratford used the tip of his index finger to push the weighty tome of a wine list toward him. "Since you're the ambitious one, you pick something."

"Okay, but don't blame me if I order something with overtones of dirt and a bouquet of shit."

"Whatever, Vinnie." Stratford rolled his eyes. "Look at this place. There's no swill in a bottle on that menu."

"Red or white?"

"Doesn't red normally go with steak? I've heard that much at least."

Vinnie snorted. "Doesn't matter much if you hate red wine or it gives you migraines or something, now does it?"

"True. I like red wine just fine."

Vinnie was tempted to just order a Chianti as usual, but the menu gave wine recommendations, so he decided on the red recommended for the strip steak he was planning to order.

They ordered, although Stratford blanched a few times reading the menu. The prices were rather steep, but the steaks had been phenomenal. He was pleased Stratford ordered neither the cheapest nor the most expensive steak on the menu, and they were able to agree on a few sides to share as accompaniments.

After their wine was poured, Stratford leaned forward and rested his elbows on the table. "So, what exactly do you do for a living?"

In a mere moment, Vinnie made a decision. His dating life hadn't been sparse due to lack of opportunity. A fair number of people, women and men both, had tried to get him to put work aside long enough to date. Sometimes he took them up on it, but he had responsibilities he couldn't ignore. Others... well, he might not have a college education, but he wasn't a fool. He wasn't stupid enough to take up with someone who only saw him as a walking debit card.

As much as he desperately wanted to believe Stratford wasn't one of those, he'd met a few who hadn't shown their true colors right away. He needed to know Stratford liked him for him, not for his money. Because he'd seen the relationship his parents had had before his dad had died. They'd never been rich but had always been happy. Vinnie had been too busy to be truly happy, not like that. He wanted happy.

"I'm an auto mechanic. I own a small shop, with a few employees." It wasn't a total lie. He still kept up his certifications, even if he hadn't been under the chassis of a customer's car in almost ten years. And he still owned his dad's small shop that had supported his family through some of the worst and leanest times in his life, but someone else managed it now.

"A mechanic. Got any overalls?" Stratford wiggled his brows, and Vinnie relaxed. There hadn't been one iota of upset over his blue-collar profession; he could handle a little fantasy about a working man.

"I might be able to dig up a pair, if you were interested." He hadn't visited the shop in a couple of months, but the thought of taking Stratford there some night, opening up one of the bays, and bending him over the hood of a car sent a wave of lust through him, which he ruthlessly suppressed. Lionel had been after him for years now to get himself a boyfriend. If Vinnie wanted to borrow the shop one evening, Lionel would look the other way. A far cry from the homophobic, narrow-minded guys his dad had originally hired for the shop.

"Maybe." Stratford's mischievous look did nothing to calm him down.

"What about you?"

Stratford shrugged. "I'm a graphic designer, sort of, for Nectar."

"Nectar? The card shop?"

"Yep. Nectar Greeting Cards and Gifts. But I work at the head office."

"How are you 'sort of' a graphic designer?"

"I went to school for graphic design, with a few courses in marketing. I started working for Nectar as soon as I graduated. I do a lot of graphic design, but I also do a mess of other jobs. I'm... in charge of one of the lines, so I do just about everything for it."

"Wow. That's sounds great."

Stratford shrugged again. "I guess. I hoped I'd be doing something else by now. But it pays the bills."

"Sometimes, that's all that matters." Vinnie knew, far too well, the truth of that.

Stratford leaned forward a little more. "Sounds like you've been there."

Pressing his lips together, Vinnie considered his dinner companion. He didn't want to depress anyone, but addressing Stratford's unspoken question dealt with the worst thing in Vinnie's life. But, it had happened a long time ago, and if Stratford was going to be a fixture in Vinnie's life, it wasn't like he'd never find out.

"My dad owned the auto-repair shop before I did. I started working there with him when I was... twelve, thirteen. Something like that. I loved the cars, I loved the shop. I apprenticed with him for a long time. He died when I was in my last year of high school, and, well, me working in the shop was the only thing that kept food on the table for a few years."

"Oh, I'm so sorry." This time it was Stratford who reached out to him, grasping his hand and giving it a comforting squeeze.

"Thanks. It was a long time ago. But... it meant I never went to college."

Stratford huffed out a laugh and leaned back again, separating their hands. Immediately, Vinnie missed the warmth of Stratford's long, strong fingers. "Take a look at this place. Even if this is only a once-in-a-blue-moon splurge, I think you're doing just fine. Better than me. I'm completely broke trying to pay off my student loans. You should see my apartment. It's tiny and pathetic."

Vinnie's voice got low again. "I'd like to see it." *Because it likely has a bed.*

A hint of Stratford's flustered fidgeting returned as he straightened his silverware. "Um, sure, maybe. Wouldn't your place be better?"

Despite the flashes of lust he'd found easier and easier to read in Stratford's eyes, he didn't sound all that enthused. Perhaps it was time for some more honesty. He didn't want to chase Stratford away, and aside from the small omission of wanting to keep his wealth a secret for the time being, he truly believed honesty was the only way to build trust.

"My place." He sighed. "Hi, I'm Vinnie Giani. I'm thirty-four, and I still live with my mother."

Stratford's eyes widened, but Vinnie continued before he had a chance to say anything.

"It's pretty common, I think. Most of the Italian guys—and girls—I know lived at home until they got married." He laughed. "They just got married long before I did."

"Does your mother ever go out?"

"Sure, sure, but my three sisters also still live at home. One's still in high school, and one's got a five-year-old daughter. Who also lives with us."

"Uh, holy estrogen bomb."

"Yeah, so the maxi pad as emergency bandage? I learned that real early."

Stratford grinned. "You don't say. I guess that explains the enormous car."

Vinnie sipped his wine. Not Chianti, but it had a smooth, robust flavor. "The Navigator was a treat for me, sure, but I did need a car big enough to lug the whole family around."

"So, I guess that also explains why you'd like to see my apartment."

"Yes, eventually," Vinnie forced himself to say.

"Not tonight?"

"No. I'm not a jump-into-bed-on-the-first-date sort of guy."

Stratford perked up a bit. "Oh?"

They were interrupted by the server bringing their meals. For a long time they concentrated on their food and the wine, both of which were excellent. Vinnie got a lot of pleasure out of Stratford's enjoyment of the meal. Perhaps a result of the training he got from his mom who equated feeding with love, or perhaps some primitive instinctive response to providing his chosen companion with sustenance, but he could watch Stratford eat every damned day.

AFTER Vinnie paid the bill, Stratford pushed away from the table, stuffed like a Thanksgiving turkey. Under normal circumstances, the amount of wine he'd had should have had him tipsy, if not outright drunk. But the steak, potatoes, creamed spinach, and broccoli had soaked up the alcohol.

Amazingly, Vinnie hadn't even hesitated when Stratford offered to pay half. Vinnie had flat out refused. Stratford never expected a free ride, but he also didn't get the sense that Vinnie was expecting him to pay for his meal with blowjobs or performing in amateur sex shows, as Barry clearly had. Stratford wasn't mercenary or he'd have found a sugar daddy a long time ago, but being treated to a fabulous meal was a real luxury; even better when it came at the hands of a sexy, compelling man who seemed interested in more than just sex.

Stratford had assumed he'd be unable to offer any man much in the way of relationship material until he got out from under all his debt, but Vinnie understood what it was like to have to work hard to survive. He just had to make sure Vinnie wouldn't judge him for his lack of funds. Vinnie seemed to have his shit together in a way Stratford could only dream of.

Being a small-business owner was awesome, but he had no idea owning an auto-repair shop could provide so well. Even though he would have been bashed right out of the class, maybe he should have paid more attention to the auto shop in high school. Despite the extravagant meal at a swanky restaurant, he hoped Vinnie was just a regular guy and not too far out of Stratford's reach.

After all, the conversation had flowed freely, as soon as they'd gotten off the topic of families. He hadn't wanted to probe too much into Vinnie's life because he wasn't interested in discussing his own family, or lack thereof.

"Want to go see a movie? There's a theater just a few blocks over."

Stratford didn't want to dismiss Vinnie's suggestion, but nor did he want the evening to end. Unfortunately, Friday and Saturday were busy nights for movie theaters, and he knew from past experience that was never a good idea.

"I don't get the chance to see movies in the theater often, but… I'm a talker. I can't sit there and just watch, I have to tell the actors they're being idiots, and I'll yell or swear or wonder why there's a plot hole the size of Rome in the story. The weekends are usually too busy for me to watch a movie without getting kicked out. Most people don't want to go with me." Never for first-run movies, anyway. Sometimes Abby would go with him to the cheapie second-run theater, but never more than a couple times a year. Which was all he could afford, anyway.

Vinnie tilted his head as though assessing an alien species. He didn't, however, run screaming. Each time Vinnie stayed through Stratford's weirdness it was another battle won, because Stratford had already decided he wasn't ditching Vinnie. Not unless Vinnie transformed into a serial killer or something. For a change, he was eager to see where they could go together, with no thought of running.

"Got it. No movies with lots of other people. What about Crabtree Park? I think this is the first night of their Christmas-light display."

"Sure, yeah, let's do that." Stratford didn't think he'd ever been on such a romantic date. Rather pathetic he'd managed to make it to almost thirty without this. Most guys were only interested in how quickly they could get him into bed. He was going to savor this as long as he could.

The temperature was a lot colder after an hour and a half in the restaurant, but he'd been fortified by meat and wine that had been so smooth going down, he and Vinnie had easily polished off the entire bottle.

They managed to make it to the park without Stratford freezing to death, and once they were among the trees it warmed up a bit. He

61

didn't know if it was because the trees shielded the wind or because the sparkling strings of lights gave off a tangible warmth when in such large clusters.

The entrance to the walking path was lit up in tiny white lights, and they followed the other few clumps of people who braved the chill to see the first night of lights. Stratford couldn't hold back his smile. It was an almost magical omen for a first date. He glanced over, only to find Vinnie watching him, an indulgent smile curving lips Stratford was getting more desperate to kiss every minute they spent together.

Vinnie stretched out a leather-gloved hand and took his uninjured left hand, making Stratford's smile even bigger. Hand in hand they meandered down the path, a glowing warmth in Stratford's chest that worked even better than meat and wine to shield him from the elements.

Vinnie squeezed his fingers briefly before speaking. "So, now that we're away from any sharp implements, I think it's safe to ask this question. What's with the bow ties?"

Blood rushed to Stratford's cheeks. It hadn't been the question that had flustered him so much but the unexpected touch from a gorgeous man he had assumed was straight. He'd been so desperate not to react in a way that would get his ass kicked that he'd managed to make a fool of himself in a completely different way.

"I like them. They're different and a bit of fun and… well…." He wasn't sure he could or should admit this. After all, he didn't really look like it, but he was a geek at heart, and Vinnie was so far from being a geek he wasn't sure he could sustain this gratifying and reciprocated interest.

"Well what? Don't get me wrong, I like them. I've just never dated anyone with them."

Vinnie steered them around a couple of kids tossing wet leaves at each other, clearly desperate for the first snowfall and snowball fight of the year.

"I love *Doctor Who*, and the current incarnation wears bow ties. I have a little crush." Stratford spit out the sentences quickly, almost running his words together.

"*Doctor Who*? I've heard of the show, but I've never seen it."

"You've never seen it? Oh, you don't know what you're missing. Sci-fi but with a hint of the ridiculous, sometimes terrifying, sometimes campy. You never know what you're going to get in an episode, and it's a lot of fun."

"Okay, then. Maybe I'll check it out." Stratford tried not to get discouraged. Wasn't the first time he'd heard that statement from guys. Usually it was just a way to change the topic because Stratford could be a bit obsessive. It was one of the few series he made a point of saving money to buy the DVDs for, since he got so much repeated watching out of them.

At the end of the path, they stood and stared up at the large evergreen that had been completely covered in a dizzying array of multicolored lights. It should have been overkill, and yet it was surprisingly beautiful. Stratford could stay here forever, holding Vinnie's hand.

They'd only been there a moment before Vinnie tugged at their clasped hands. Stratford had been ready to protest that he wasn't ready to move on until he saw Vinnie was directing them away from the main viewing area around the brightly lit Christmas tree centerpiece and into a natural alcove created by the corner of a hedge.

As they stood close together, Vinnie's body warmed Stratford's front, and their breath mingled. Vinnie bit the finger of his glove and tugged it off. Despite the sensation of being in their own little cocoon, rife with sensual promise, the boyish gesture made Stratford giggle. The giggling stopped when Vinnie stroked the side of Stratford's face with his bare hand. Apparently fascinated by the slight rasp of stubble Stratford had forgotten to shave, Vinnie continued to rub a finger along his jawline.

Each stroke made him shiver, and blood, sluggish with cold, migrated south.

"So tell me, Stratford Dale." Vinnie's fingers slipped lower, a ghost of sensation on his neck, before the tip of Vinnie's index finger slid between collar and neck, the sensation surprisingly erotic. His voice had also dropped, as it had a time or two, to a deep rumble that triggered little flutters of desire in Stratford's belly and balls. "Are these clip-on bow ties, or are they real ones? Ones that I can grip one

63

end, slowly pull on it, and watch it untie like unwrapping a present, all for me?"

"Oh, I'm a present you can unwrap." Stratford didn't even flush when he said it, because there was no mistaking Vinnie's look, not this close up.

Vinnie slipped his finger out of Stratford's shirt and moved to cup the back of his head, tilting it just enough to let their lips meet, like a perfectly choreographed dance.

Vinnie kept the kiss light, lip-to-lip, for a few seconds. Then he slipped his tongue out and pressed for entrance. Parting his lips, Stratford allowed Vinnie to deepen the kiss, then slid his tongue along Vinnie's. Their breath came quicker, the heated humidity skimming over his cheek. Stratford had never been kissed like this—erotically charged yet the sweetest thing ever.

Stratford pressed himself closer, but only succeeded in mashing his erection to his body. With both of their coats in the way, he couldn't feel any tangible proof of Vinnie's arousal. The hands rubbing along his back had an urgent note to them, and when Vinnie dropped his hands to Stratford's ass, grinding them together, Stratford knew, even if he couldn't feel it, that Vinnie was aching as much as he was.

The tinkle of laughter made them spring apart. Panting, they scanned the area, but no one was actually looking at them, merely the sounds of the public intruding on their little bubble of alone-ness.

"Sorry, I didn't mean to do that."

Stratford frowned. Vinnie hadn't meant to kiss him? "So, what, you tripped and fell on my mouth?"

Vinnie laughed and slipped his glove on. "No, the kiss wasn't an accident. I meant to kiss you. I've wanted to since the first time I saw you."

He had? Another flutter of desire took up residence in Stratford's belly, erasing his upset at Vinnie's poorly chosen words.

"Me too."

Vinnie touched Stratford's lower lip with a finger, a whiff of leather drifting into Stratford's nose. "Good. But I didn't mean for it to get so...."

"Hot?" Stratford's quirked brow and question made Vinnie shake his head and laugh again.

"No, hot was good. Hot was hoped for. But it went a little further than I'd intended."

"In public?" Stratford cursed his unruly mouth for spilling out the first thing that came to mind. But he really, really didn't want Vinnie to be embarrassed by him, or by them together.

Vinnie raised an eyebrow. "Oh, I don't much care about that, either. Before you managed to cut yourself, I had a fantasy or two of you spread out on one of those cooking stations. Just the right height, for a number of things."

Stratford sucked in a breath, the blood pounding into his groin no longer sluggish as he imagined what sort of things Vinnie could do to him on those tables. He stepped closer and tipped his head, angling for another kiss.

Irritatingly, Vinnie stepped back again. "See, now, I did it again. I want to get to know you. Before we have sex. It's our first date, and I hadn't intended for things to get so intense."

With an exaggerated shake of his hips, Stratford pressed himself up against Vinnie again. "Don't you think it's important to know early if we're compatible?"

Vinnie snorted. "Is there some question about that?"

Before Stratford could blink, Vinnie had worked his hand underneath Stratford's coat and had a deliciously firm grip of his cock. With a muted whimper, he bucked his hips, trying for a little more pressure, a little more sensation. If it weren't so cold, he'd wish his pants were open.

"Think we're not compatible?" Vinnie taunted him.

"No, no." Stratford bucked again, but Vinnie had already removed his hand. "No! Now I just think you're an asshole for teasing me." There was no heat in his tone and Vinnie knew it.

"C'mon. Let's go check out the theatre anyway, because you're freezing, and I don't want to take you home just yet."

"I'm not freezing." Now that Vinnie was no longer providing full-body warmth, Stratford had to consciously keep his teeth from chattering.

Vinnie kissed his nose, which truth be told, was nearly numb. "Liar. I don't want you losing any parts to frostbite."

"If you took me home, I'd let you come in. You could warm me up."

"No, no sex."

Stratford grinned. If Vinnie had wound him up enough that there might be blue balls in his future, at least he had the satisfaction of knowing Vinnie was going to be in equal discomfort.

"Fine. Are you sure about the movie, though?"

"We'll find something unpopular enough to keep you out of trouble. There's bound to be something. And if I'm wrong, well, I've never gotten tossed from a movie before. Be a new experience."

"Okay, but don't say I didn't warn you."

Vinnie opened his mouth but closed it again.

"What?"

"Nothing. I'll tell you on… our third date."

Stratford wiggled. That meant whatever thought had passed through Vinnie's mind was something fucking sexy. More importantly, Vinnie wanted to get to three dates. And he was a damn sight better than the half-hearted relationship he'd had with Nik that had fizzled out after a couple of months.

This time, Vinnie wrapped an arm around Stratford's shoulder and tugged him close before leading them out of the park.

Five

AFTER Stratford had almost plowed into a couple of people on the sidewalk—Vinnie having pulled him out of the collision's path—he shook himself out of his euphoric haze to pay attention to his surroundings. Down the street, perhaps another two or three blocks, the neon-accented, classic-style marquee was clearly visible. It lit a different sort of excitement in his chest. Movies weren't a good use of his disposable income, not when he was usually asked to leave, so he only rarely went. Abby would occasionally go with him, but she always got mad when they were kicked out. He'd managed to avoid early dating mishaps by not going. Even the few boyfriends he'd had soon learned to go to the movies with their friends and leave him at home. The fact that Vinnie didn't seem to care one way or the other dissolved a lot of the trepidation he felt when attending a movie with someone.

He had to give Vinnie one last out. "Are you sure you want to do this? What if we miss the end of the movie? I usually have to wait until they come out on cable to see how they end."

Vinnie shrugged, not letting go of Stratford's hand. "Until recently, I didn't really have time to go to the movies. I'm not invested in the ending, and honestly, I'll probably have a lot more fun teasing you about getting kicked out than I will about finding out for sure the guy manages to get the girl or everyone dies or everyone's already dead."

"Cool."

A guy with dark, perfectly groomed hair caught Stratford's eyes, about fifty feet in front of them, standing in line for a club, based on everyone's clothing. He looked a little familiar, but it wasn't until he turned his head to talk to his companion that Stratford realized it was Barry the Biter with his new, presumably plugged squeeze, Trey. Panic pushed adrenaline through his system, making him a little light-headed.

Vinnie was walking fast, and Stratford didn't know how to avoid passing the line they'd be upon within moments.

"Wait." Stratford yanked on Vinnie's hand and pulled him into a darkened shop entrance between two display windows.

"What's wrong?"

"Can we go… around? Or another way?"

"Why?"

Stratford fidgeted a bit, trying to avoid Vinnie's piercing gaze.

"Hey. Come on now. We're both adults here, what's up there?"

The hint of exasperation in Vinnie's tone, when he'd been so great about everything so far, was like a bucket of cold water over Stratford's head. Stratford had no burning desire to cross paths with Barry again, but he was acting childishly. Just as childishly as Barry had been when he'd shared the details of their horrible date with everyone and lied about it.

"Just a guy I went on a date with, before I met you. It didn't go well, and I… well, I don't much like confrontations."

"It went bad enough that, what, he's going to want to punch you?"

Unwillingly, Stratford let a bleat of laughter escape. "No, I don't mean like that. I mean, like…." Stratford ramped up his inner drag queen, thrust his hip out and waved his hand around. "I mean, like, you raging bitch!" Stratford rocked the falsetto when he wanted too, but Vinnie's lips didn't even twitch. In fact, he looked almost angry.

"Do you still want to date him? Are you sorry you're out with me instead of him?"

The cold of the night had somehow invaded Vinnie's words, and he drew back, stiff and untouchable. Hurt.

Stratford's happiness crumbled. He'd been so intent on avoiding Barry at work, it seemed natural to do the same thing here on the street, where his appearance was unexpected and unwelcome. It never occurred to him that Vinnie might view his actions negatively. Which meant he had to be a man and not an ostrich for once in his miserable life.

This time, he was the one who stripped off his gloves to cup Vinnie's strong, square jaw.

"Believe me, you're a far better man. I was thrilled when you asked me out. And if it makes you feel better, my date with him was so bad, I told him I was getting a drink at the bar, and then I just kept walking." Some of the tight lines of tension around Vinnie's eyes eased, but Stratford wasn't out of the woods yet. Fortunately, he still had one ace in the hole. "I walked past the community center, and I stopped to watch a cooking class. I saw a gorgeous, sexy man, and I went home, figured out what class it was, then signed up."

Comprehension lit Vinnie's eyes. "That was you. I turned around and thought I saw a guy wearing a bow tie in the window."

"Yeah, you kinda scared me. I tripped and fell." Stratford pulled the hand that wasn't bandaged away from Vinnie's face and brandished it at him, with a few healed scrapes still visible. The final remnants of pain disappeared from Vinnie's face, and he dipped his head to place gentle kisses on Stratford's palm.

Then Vinnie pulled him into another searing, full-body kiss, nibbling on his bottom lip before finally pulling away. Vinnie's hands dropped to Stratford's pockets, and for a split second, Stratford thought they'd get to pick up where they left off, but Vinnie merely pulled out his shitty gloves. He hated them, but they did the job—mostly—and he couldn't justify spending money on another pair until these ones got lost or fell apart.

"Put these back on. It's too cold to go without." Vinnie's voice was soft and caring, and Stratford got a momentary heart-melting flash of him taking care of younger sisters. The sweetness of it was almost unbearable, considering he did his level best to ignore the fact he had family who didn't want anything to do with him.

Vinnie dropped kisses along Stratford's neck and ears while he struggled to put on his gloves. The distraction of Vinnie destroyed his concentration. After fumbling for a few seconds, he was finally gloved to Vinnie's satisfaction, who grabbed his hand again.

"C'mon. Head up. If you're happy to be with me, don't be afraid to show it—to anyone and everyone."

Hand in hand, they stepped back out onto the main thoroughfare and walked toward the movie theater.

As Stratford had feared, Barry turned at the wrong time and saw him. With Vinnie at his side, though, it was amazingly easy not to flinch.

"Well, well, well. Look, Trey, it's Stratford." Barry the Biter elbowed Trey the Twink, and the two just smirked at him.

"Oh, you two are on another date? Good for you," Stratford said. He wanted to make some snide remark about how stretched Trey was, but mostly he wanted to forget about that horrible date. If Trey didn't mind wearing a plug so he could get gangbanged as the centerpiece in a sex show, well, he and Barry deserved each other.

As though Trey had heard Stratford's thoughts, he moved closer to Barry and wrapped their arms together. Barry, however, had spied Vinnie connected to the end of Stratford's arm and was giving him the once over.

Then he shook his head sadly and gave Vinnie the most insincere sympathetic expression Stratford had ever seen. "You should just give up now, he's a bit of a prude. Any money you spent on him was wasted."

"Virgin," Trey hissed, as though it was some sort of disease.

Stratford stood and gaped, as did a few of the other people in line who had no trouble overhearing their spiteful words. Again, he wondered if he'd been transported back to high school. He wanted to defend himself, but stamping his foot and exclaiming that he wasn't a virgin didn't seem like a dignified response. This was why he just wanted to avoid the whole encounter altogether.

Vinnie squared those broad shoulders, which Stratford now knew to have been developed through many years as an auto mechanic, and stepped between him and Barry. He was only an inch or so taller than Stratford's six feet, but they both topped Barry by a couple of inches, and although muscular, Barry didn't have anything like Vinnie's muscles. He positively loomed over Barry and Trey, who was built like a true twink.

"Hello, my name's Vincent. I'd rather you didn't presume to know what my preferences were, nor to advise me on dating. It's not polite. Got it, kid?"

Vinnie's voice was soft and even, but Stratford shivered at the menace dripping from the fairly innocuous words, even though they weren't directed at him. Barry and Trey both shrank back, and the people on either side of them in line shuffled away, clearly intent on letting the Biter and the Twink take the brunt of Vinnie's displeasure.

"C'mon, hon, let's go." Vinnie tucked him close and ushered him on.

Although Stratford wasn't sure how he felt letting Vinnie take the encounter over the way he did, Stratford had only one option open. To make sure his happiness at being with Vinnie was clear on his face. He wouldn't want Barry to mistake it for anything else. Moving away, Stratford stood tall, proudly hand in hand with Vinnie.

Stratford couldn't stop grinning. He might get some shit at work, but he rarely needed to speak to Trey, and Barry, well, Barry wasn't anywhere even close to Vinnie, which Stratford had been fully aware of but just needed the extra nudge Vinnie gave him to realize that meant confrontation might sometimes be a good thing.

When Vinnie found a crappy horror movie that had been out for a few weeks and as a result had a nearly empty theatre, he was almost giddy. This man... this one he could fall for. Maybe he already had.

VINNIE pulled into the medical center parking lot, maneuvered to a spot in the shadows, and put the car in park, but he didn't turn the car off. He'd had a great time with Stratford. Better than he'd even expected. And yet, there was the tiny incident with Barry, Stratford's last date before meeting Vinnie. Over and over during the movie, his mind had returned to it, like an aching tooth he couldn't stop probing with his tongue. As comfortable as he felt with Stratford already, and the belief deep in his gut that Stratford was worth getting to know, he still didn't know what made Stratford tick. Stratford had confirmed he didn't like confrontation, but the almost manic avoidance and knee-jerk reaction to run had to have some deeper cause, and he wanted to know what it was.

Stratford's words had calmed him at the time, but the more he thought about Barry, the more insecure he got. For the first time in his life, it mattered—deeply—whether someone truly wanted to be with him. And if Stratford held some lingering desire to be with Barry, Vinnie was going to have to call this off before his heart got too tangled up. He'd seen his mother's devastation after his father's death, and the various heartbreaks his sisters had experienced, and he was damn sure he didn't want to undergo that. He might not have been to college, but after ten years of owning a growing business with several employees, he knew plenty about return on investment, and if he was going to invest in Stratford, he didn't want his only return to be a trampled heart.

"About that guy, Barry…." Vinnie wasn't quite sure how to ask what he wanted to know. Wasn't sure how to explain why he couldn't stop thinking about how much Stratford's reaction had hurt.

Stratford sighed, but the sound wasn't exasperated, as Vinnie had half expected him to be. The snap of the seat belt unbuckling preceded Stratford pulling up a leg and twisting in his seat to face Vinnie over the console. In response, Vinnie pushed his own seat back as far as it would go, and shifted so he could easily look into Stratford's eyes.

"I was hoping I wouldn't have to tell you this."

Vinnie's stomach dropped as Stratford's words pierced his chest. This was it. Stratford was going to tell him it was over, that he wanted that runt Barry. Barry was younger and probably way cooler than Vinnie, who'd had to be family provider and pseudofather before he'd even finished high school.

"I see."

Stratford reached out a hand, placed it on Vinnie's arm. It took everything he had not to flinch, but he tensed underneath Stratford's touch, earning him a tiny frown.

"I don't think you do. It was humiliating. I don't really want to get into too many details, but Barry and I flirted quite a bit before he asked me out. He works in the same building I do. The guy's younger than me, young enough that I wasn't sure if we'd have anything in common, but he was cute and nice, and I had high expectations." Stratford cleared his throat and dropped his gaze to his fingers and saw that he was stroking the creases on the arm of Vinnie's leather jacket.

"It's okay. You don't have to explain." The last thing he wanted to hear was details of Stratford with another guy. He'd never had a reason to feel possessive of anyone, and he worried about the dark anger coiling in his gut.

"Maybe I do. I know I didn't react well tonight, and I'm sorry for that. It's just, well, we went to dinner at a fairly nice place. Halfway through, not only did he make assumptions about my preferred uh… sexual… position, he, uh…."

Vinnie ground his teeth together. He didn't want to hear this, but short of being rude and likely killing any chance of changing Stratford's mind about Barry, he didn't know how he was going to shut Stratford up.

"Well, he asked if I was wearing a plug."

Vinnie hadn't expected to hear that. "Over dinner? Like, while you were eating? On a first date?"

Stratford nodded in response to each question, and Vinnie's incredulity and anger increased with each moment. This time, though, his anger had a focus—Barry for being such an obnoxious twit.

"That's… um…." Vinnie had absolutely no idea how to respond to that. He'd come across more than one guy who'd arrived at a club plugged and ready for action, but it would never have occurred to him to ask anyone while negotiating bathroom or alley. And if you were in a relationship with some idea of how things were going to play out, talking of plugs and such might be considered foreplay, but Vinnie couldn't imagine how that could possibly come up as anyone's idea of reasonable first-date dinner conversation. He forced his fingers to relax once they realized they'd started to curl into fists.

"So, I take it that's when you left?"

Stratford's laugh was bitter and self-deprecating. "It's been a while since I've been on a date, so I stuck it out until we got to the club."

What was the matter with the gay men in this city that Stratford hadn't been out on a date in a while? It certainly worked to Vinnie's advantage in this case, but aside from how much he enjoyed Stratford's company and learning his geeky little quirks, he'd wanted to strip the man naked from the second he saw him. Vinnie should have had to wade through a line of guys trying to get into Stratford's pants.

"And then you left?" Perhaps it wasn't the nicest thing for anyone to do, but clearly Barry had been oblivious.

"Well, not exactly." Stratford flushed again, and Vinnie had a bad feeling about his next words. "We messed around a bit. It wasn't... good."

Vinnie's nostrils flared, and the coil of anger pulsed darker and hotter than before. He wanted to believe Stratford was telling him the truth, but since they hadn't done anything but kiss, Stratford didn't know if Vinnie would be just as *not good* as Barry.

"And—"

That last word was enough to finally exasperate Stratford enough that his irritation outweighed his reticence.

"Vinnie, please trust me. There's no way I want to date Barry. Trey is fucking welcome to him. When we got to the club, I found out it wasn't just a dance club, and it was amateur sex night. Barry had signed us up for one of the slots, and I was supposed to be the filling of a Barry and an as-yet-undisclosed-Barry's-friend sandwich. In front of an audience. Even if he'd asked my permission and if my job wouldn't be in jeopardy if anyone found out... that's not me. Threesomes make great fantasies, but I've never wanted one for real, and fucking in public? No. Not a chance."

With each word, Stratford's eyes flashed, the tension in his voice matching the anger that now flared brightly in Vinnie's chest. This time, Vinnie let his fingers curl into tight fists.

"I want to go back there and punch his head in." The unfamiliar need for violence startled him. He'd been in his fair share of fights when he was younger—his dad's death had put a lot of pressure on him that needed an outlet for the first few months. But even when Gabriella got pregnant, he hadn't felt this searing need to bash something. Of course, Sienna's dad had been as young as Gabriella had been, and when they'd realized what had happened, the two of them had been petrified. Vinnie had been upset, but not filled with rage.

"Hey, no." Stratford smoothed long fingers over Vinnie's whitened knuckles. "I should have done a lot of things differently, but Barry's not worth another thought, much less an arrest. I might not need someone to fight my battles for me, but I do appreciate what you did. And I'm sorry you thought for a minute I wished I was with Barry instead of you. I'm…." Stratford's gaze dropped again. "I'm not good at talking about how I feel."

Vinnie suspected that went hand in hand with Stratford's instinct to flee at the first sign of conflict, but there'd be time to solve that issue later. He relaxed, his anger dissipating with every stroke of Stratford's fingers against his skin.

"I'm glad I met you. I know this is our first date, and I don't want to scare you off, but tonight has been the best night I've had in a long time. I want… I hope… I'd like to keep seeing you."

There was no mistaking the painful truth in Stratford's words, and the last of Vinnie's insecurity about Barry and how Stratford felt about him disappeared. They were both heading for the same destination, and they were looking to get there together.

"Same here." The separation of the console was suddenly too far. Vinnie dragged Stratford over the console and fitted him over his lap, knees pressed into the seat on either side of Vinnie's hips. Startled was an adorable look on Stratford, but Vinnie didn't think Stratford would approve of adorable any more than he would cute. He unbuttoned both of their jackets so they could at least enjoy each other's body heat without vinyl and leather in the way.

Vinnie pressed a quick kiss to Stratford's slightly parted lips. "But you're wrong about one thing. This is definitely our second date. Cooking class was our first."

Stratford blinked. "It was?"

"Oh, yes, I think it counts. We're in second-date territory." Vinnie cupped Stratford's head and brought their lips together. This time, the heated sweetness of their previous kisses morphed immediately into a fiery passion that had their tongues sliding slickly along each other as they devoured each other's mouth. Sweet mother of God, if Stratford could suck his tongue like that, he could only imagine how incredible that mouth would feel wrapped around his dick.

In seconds, Vinnie's cock was hard and pulsing. He ground his hips into Stratford, who was equally aroused and squirming against him. For a moment, he thought he could kiss Stratford until he died from lack of breath, but then Stratford huffed a moan into his mouth along with his tongue, ramping them up to a new level of arousal. The heat between them was enough to make Vinnie lose his mind, and he wanted nothing more than to strip Stratford bare right there in his car and plunge his cock into Stratford's ass.

One hand dropped to Stratford's oh-so-tempting butt, and his fingers curled around it, deliberately edging into the crack as best he could while Stratford was still wearing pants. If there was room for more than a dime down the waistband, Vinnie would have tucked his hand right down for a feel of bare buttock.

Stratford moaned louder as Vinnie increased his grip, pressing them closer together. Pulling back, Stratford stared down at him, lips moist and full, eyes glittering with wild arousal.

"If this is a second date, are you going to come upstairs?"

Vinnie bit back an agonized groan of his own. He wanted nothing more, but he'd been serious about getting to know each other without the sex. Calling this a second date hadn't been just a ploy to coerce Stratford into bed.

He wasn't ready to give up the pleasure of Stratford in his arms. Not just yet. "Nope. We're gonna kiss a little longer, then you're going to go upstairs alone and dream of me."

Stratford clearly hadn't been expecting that answer, and Vinnie took advantage of him trying to sort his fevered brain into some semblance of logic. With the hand not currently flexing and rubbing Stratford's ass Vinnie gripped Stratford's shoulder-length hair and tipped his head back, baring his throat. Vinnie was able to control himself for a few moments while he licked the smooth throat all the way up to the slightly rough chin where Stratford's stubble was just beginning to come in from his last shave. Then he licked along Stratford's narrow jaw and nuzzled his nose under an ear. Stratford wasn't wearing cologne or aftershave, and Vinnie was able to fill his nose with the undiluted, undisguised musky scent of warm, aroused male.

He slid his tongue over the vein pulsing in Stratford's neck in time with his rapid heartbeat. The realization that the veins in Stratford's erection were doing the exact same thing and the desire to have Stratford's cock in his mouth right now snapped Vinnie's control. He latched his mouth onto Stratford's neck, biting and sucking as fiercely as he'd kissed Stratford's mouth. This time, Stratford's moans weren't muffled by Vinnie's tongue, and the auditory stimulus only made him wilder. He forced a finger down the back of Stratford's pants, finding his pucker and pressing while he sucked.

Stratford's whole body stiffened before he called out Vinnie's name and his body shook with helpless spasms. Stunned, Vinnie lifted his mouth and stared up at Stratford. The aroused flush, slumberous eyelids, and warmth spreading across his crotch told the story. Hot. So fucking hot.

He'd made Stratford come in his pants. Putting the event into words, even in his own mind, pushed Vinnie over an edge he hadn't realized was there. He pulled Stratford's orgasm-slack mouth down over his and thrust his hips up, letting his own orgasm flood over him as he fucked Stratford's mouth with his tongue.

Panting, he broke the kiss and wrapped his arms around Stratford, cuddling him as best he could while they were squished together in the driver's seat of his car. He hadn't meant to go so far, but he couldn't muster up enough energy to be upset by it. Not when a fully clothed orgasm with Stratford had been better than any other he'd had in recent memory.

"I'm pretty sure coming in our pants is a second-base activity not a second-date activity," Stratford mumbled into his neck.

Vinnie let out a lazy chuckle. "Yeah, I hadn't intended to go so far."

"But it was good."

Clutching Stratford tighter, Vinnie smiled. "So fucking good."

"You want to come up now? Clean up a bit?" Stratford tensed a bit before he spoke. "Stay the night?"

"I don't want to rush this. And I don't want my mother to worry."

He'd no sooner got the words out when it was as though he was cuddling a cat that didn't want to be held. No claws but all sharp angles and stiff muscles.

"What's wrong?"

"Your mother? You... have to check in with her?"

Vinnie could only imagine how it sounded. At thirty-four, worried about staying out all night without his mother's permission, he probably sounded one short step away from Norman Batesville. He did his best to soothe Stratford by yanking his shirt out of his pants and rubbing the warm supple skin of his back.

"Yes and no. My mother doesn't mind if I stay out all night. I don't need permission, but if she wakes up tomorrow and I'm not there, she'll worry. It's too late to call her and... I told you I have a seventeen-year-old sister, right?"

Stratford nodded into his chest without looking up.

"I have to set a good example. My sister, Evie, she was only one when my dad died. She doesn't have any memories of him. I'm the closest thing she's got to a father, and I have to act like a responsible adult for her benefit."

The stiff angles of Stratford's body melted when he started laughing. "Instead of a horny teenager doling out hickeys and coming in his pants."

Hickeys? "Oh, shit." He tipped Stratford's neck back, and the unmistakable signature of a hickey was visible even in the dim light of the vehicle's interior. "I'm sorry, you should have said something."

Stratford laughed even more. "I did. I'm pretty sure I screamed your name as I came. What else should I have said?"

Despite his spent cock and the swamp in his crotch, the memory of the primal pleasure he'd experienced when Stratford came apart so unexpectedly in his arms made him want to do it all over again.

"I'd better get going." Vinnie had to leave or Stratford would be able to beguile him out of his good intentions with those puffy, kiss-swollen lips and wide brown eyes. "Are you free tomorrow night?"

He'd phrased it as a question, but if Stratford had other plans with another guy, he might just lose his mind. The way he felt right now, he could easily see himself spending every night for the foreseeable future with Stratford, and not only to discover the many ways he could tip Stratford over into orgasm.

Stratford frowned. "Can we play it by ear? I have this work thing I have to do tomorrow. My boss just sprung it on me this week, and I'm afraid I'll be exhausted afterward." The frown disappeared and his lips quirked up at the corners. "I'd like to be fully energized for our next date."

"Is it anything I can help with?" The extra number of hours in his week after hiring his sister was almost alarming. Having evenings and weekends free was a pleasure, but he sometimes wondered what to do to fill up the time.

Stratford shook his head. "I wish, but no. It's a last-minute project to gear up for the Christmas rush, and since it involves my line, I'm stuck doing it."

"Okay, then. I'll probably do some stuff with the family tomorrow during the day. Call me when you're done and we'll see how you feel. Maybe I'll tell my mom I won't be home." He winked at Stratford.

"Sounds like a plan." Stratford kissed him, and Vinnie opened his door. With some undignified shifting, they managed to untangle themselves from each other, and Stratford stumbled out of the car, righting himself before he fell to the ground.

"You okay?"

Stratford rolled his eyes and held up his hands, palm out, displaying both scrapes and the bandage covering his stitches.

"Yes, but that's why my hands are like this." His devilish look returned. "I should probably thank you. The stitches make it hard to...." Stratford made an obscene gesture mimicking jacking off, and Vinnie laughed.

"Anytime, Stratford, anytime."

With an exaggerated flounce and shimmy of his hips that had Vinnie drooling, Stratford let himself into his building. Vinnie didn't shut his car door until Stratford's door had closed behind him. He'd forgotten to ask if Stratford had any roommates, but if they got together tomorrow, Vinnie would spring for a hotel room if needed. Third date was plenty of time to discover each other naked.

THE ringing of his phone pulled Stratford out of a pleasant fantasy about Vinnie. He'd been ready to take himself in hand, but then he remembered his right hand was still sore and stitched. Damn. Might as well answer the phone.

Abby. He fumbled to answer it with his left hand.

"Hey, Abby."

"Get up, lazy bones. It's almost noon. You're not spending another weekend wallowing in your apartment. I'm kidnapping you for the day."

Stratford fell back on his bed and groaned. Abby on a mission was exhausting, but he'd much rather be subjected to her good intentions than doing what he had to do today.

"Abby, seriously, I can't. I have to work."

"Work? What the hell? Have those bastards at Nectar finally instituted sweatshop hours? We both know they want to."

"Pretty much, yeah." Tomorrow he might be able to laugh about it, but today, the yoke of his job lay heavy on his neck. "I have to do a public reading as Doctor Chicken this afternoon, and I will definitely be spending the rest of the weekend hiding out in my apartment."

"Those bastards. You really need to get a new job. I bet you don't even get flextime for working on the weekend." Abby hated his job more than he did.

"They said I would." But Stratford didn't believe that, either.

"Where are you going to be? I'll come out and watch."

Anxiety knotted his stomach. "No, Abby, please. I think I'd be more nervous if you were there."

"Okay, if you're sure. Let me know how it goes. Are you still coming over for Thanksgiving dinner?"

"I should be able to leave the office early, but I still might be a little late."

Abby's irritated sigh floated loud over the phone. "Someone else needs to take over that shift for a change. You've done it every year since you started there."

With the stress of the weekend reading event hanging over his head, Stratford found it harder to come up with his usual defenses for his job.

"I know having someone in the office in case there are emergencies is total bullshit. No greeting-card emergency has happened. Never in the history of ever."

He stared up at the stains on his bedroom ceiling, left over from a roof leak a few years ago. If only he could see the face of Jesus or Mother Theresa, he might have been able to make some money from it.

"But Abby, working on Thanksgiving just makes it easier to forget." He didn't need to tell her what he wanted to forget. She knew. When his parents disowned him, he lost his entire family. The focus of Christmas had been split between religion and family, but Thanksgiving had pretty much been all about family when he was growing up, and although Abby was the best friend he could hope for, Thanksgiving was hard.

Her voice softened. "Yeah, I know."

Stratford couldn't stand the depressing tone of their conversation. Not if he was going to be swarmed by hordes of kids later.

"I had a date last night."

There was a stunned pause while Abby assimilated the abrupt change of subject.

"Not that Barry guy again. Stratford, you need to let me set you up."

"No, not Barry. How fucking desperate do you think I am?" Stratford didn't pause because he didn't want to find out the answer. "It was a guy I met at cooking class."

"You signed up for that class for a guy, didn't you?"

Abby could disapprove all she wanted. "Maybe, but he did ask me out."

"Really? The same guy you were after?"

"Yep, turns out he wasn't straight after all." Stratford groaned. He hadn't meant to admit he'd impulsively registered for the class because he couldn't stop thinking about the hot Italian guy he'd assumed was straight.

"Stratford…. Okay, so tell me all about it."

"Can't, Abby. I have to get ready for my… event."

"Wait, are you going to call him?"

"I told you, after this ridiculous event is over, I'm coming home and staying in bed for the rest of the weekend."

"Fine. But we're going to talk later. Good luck this afternoon."

Stratford disconnected. He wasn't in that much of a rush, but for the same reason he hadn't immediately texted Abby as soon as Vinnie had asked him on the date, he wasn't sure he wanted to talk about him yet. The night had been special, and he didn't want to jinx it. If Vinnie called him for a second date, maybe he'd be less superstitious about it.

Six

VINNIE sat at the kitchen table, a cup of coffee and a plate of toast at one elbow, his Kindle in front of him. He had too much energy to read all day, but he didn't have one single plan for the day or night, except to hope Stratford called him after his work thing.

He rubbed his belly. Maybe a visit to the gym wouldn't hurt. When he'd worked the shop regularly, he hadn't needed a gym. Working with the cars and parts had been exercise aplenty, but the cushy office life had softened his stomach. He was careful, and he didn't have love handles—yet. He'd merely lost any definition on his belly.

Regretting the cooking class that led him to Stratford was out of the question. He'd love to cook for Stratford someday soon, and he had a feeling Stratford wouldn't care if the only thing he knew how to cook was Italian.

A piercing squeal broke the lazy silence of an early Saturday morning in the Giani household. Vinnie's niece was awake and happy about something. Upset and happy, although both loud and in an almost painful range of sound, were very different vocalizations. Happy was always better.

Little feet pounded along the hall upstairs to the staircase, heading inexorably toward him. Or the kitchen. Could be either. Sienna's motivations still sometimes escaped him, much as her mother's had at that age.

She skidded into the kitchen, still dressed in pink pajamas, and Vinnie leapt out his chair, ready to catch her.

"Shouldn't be running in the house, little girl. I'm pretty sure me, Nonna, and your mother have told you that before."

The reprimand didn't even register. Sienna's eyes burned with the fervor of an addict or zealot. She held a crumpled piece of newspaper in her small fist, and she lifted it toward him. Confused, Vinnie took it.

"Mama said you could take me. Please, Uncle Vinnie, please!" Sienna danced in place, so excited she was doing the pee-pee dance. Vinnie hoped she wasn't actually that excited.

"Where do you want to go?"

"Doctor Chicken!"

He wasn't going to get any sense out of her, but whatever it was, Gabriella had decided to foist the outing on Vinnie, whether he wanted to go or not. Smoothing out the paper, he pored over it, trying to find whatever had Sienna bouncing off the walls.

A quarter-page ad in yellow and red provided the answer. Doctor Chicken, the author of Sienna's favorite series of books, was doing an inaugural reading and autograph session at a nearby Nectar store.

"You want to go hear Doctor Chicken."

"And get an autograph." Sienna sighed, the sound precocious and probably what he'd hear in a few years when boy bands or teen actors caught her attention. He hadn't even realized Sienna knew what an autograph was.

Still, if he did this…. "Go get your mama. After I talk to her, I'll let you know if we're going to go."

"Please," she whined, the sound putting his teeth on edge. He loved his niece, but there was no avoiding it—some of her habits, or those of any young girl, could be incredibly irritating.

"Sienna." He infused a little command in his tone. "Please do as I ask, or there will be zero chance of a Doctor Chicken visit."

She pushed out a trembling lower lip but stamped back upstairs. Gabriella had probably been hoping to make it all Uncle Vinnie's problem while she turned over and went back to sleep. *Not a chance, little sis.*

A good fifteen minutes later, Gabriella stumbled into the kitchen. She was the only one of them who wasn't a morning person. "Vinnie, can't you take her? Everyone's busy today, and I've got a paper to write."

Like he was going to deny his spoiled little niece anything. But a negotiation never hurt. "On one condition. Someone else takes her to see Santa."

Gabriella rolled her eyes, but Vinnie wasn't going to budge. He loved Sienna like his own daughter, but the horde of screaming kids was a horror a single adorable photo of Sienna on the jolly old elf's lap couldn't combat. The Doctor Chicken reading would undoubtedly be just as awful, and there was no way Vinnie was doing it twice in a year. If he thought he could have wrung the concession out of her, he'd have bargained to get out of playing chauffeur on Black Friday, too, but his other sisters would probably lynch him if he tried.

"I mean it, Gabriella. I'll do it, but I'm out for Santa. Got it?"

"Yeah, sure. No Santa." She trudged out of the kitchen, undoubtedly heading for the haven of her bed. On her way, she yelled out to Sienna. "He said he'd do it."

Seconds later, Sienna was back at his side, bouncing and hugging him.

"Yeah, yeah." He glanced at the time. Too bad it wasn't soon. Sienna acting as though she was on a sugar high until after lunch would be an ordeal in itself. "Why don't you go decide which of your Doctor Chicken books is your favorite? You can take it with you to get autographed, okay?"

Surprisingly, that was enough. He knew from past experience she had a hard time determining which was her favorite, so it might keep her occupied for a couple of hours at least, even if it meant having every single one of the floppy books strewn about the floor of her bedroom before she decided.

I'M FREAKING the fuck out.

Stratford hit Send and pocketed his phone. He paced the Nectar store's employee lounge while waiting for Abby to respond to his text.

The place was about as loungy as his apartment was luxury accommodations. How was it, exactly, that Nectar had any employees at all? Worse than the cubicle farm back at the office.

He'd gotten there an hour early, even though there was very little for him to set up, since the store's cashiers had already rearranged the displays to make room for him and his tiny minions, as well as posted signs informing customers of his impending appearance.

Glancing in the smudged and scratched mirror provided in the lounge allowed the cashiers to return to work after lunch without poppy seeds in their teeth. Stratford used it to readjust his bow tie. Remembering Vinnie's pleasure in the bow tie, despite the fact that the man had—unbelievably—never watched *Doctor Who*, produced the first smile since he'd left his apartment today. Thinking about Vinnie relaxed him but also got him hot, and he had no intention of going out into throngs of kidlets and parents all fired up from remembering his date last night.

The phone in his pocket vibrated with a text notification, making him jump.

I can still get there before you start.

Stratford shook his head as he started typing, even though Abby couldn't see him.

No. I'll be more nervous if I see someone I know. I feel dorky enough doing this.

Those kids already love you. You'll be a hit. Don't stress. Come over after for drinks.

I don't want to be a hit. You know that. No drinks—I told you, I'm just going sleep for the rest of the weekend.

Fine. But you should listen to me and quit. If you can't find something right away, you know I'll help out.

Stratford wasn't going to have this argument with Abby again. He could handle the job for three more years. Then, even if he had to start somewhere at rock bottom, at least he'd still be able to afford rent and food.

Gotta go. Have stuff to get ready.

He turned off his phone so he didn't have to be distracted by her inevitable reply, pressuring him to quit. Once that door was opened, it was tough to get her to give it a rest. Lately, it seemed any mention of his job at all had her trying to convince him to quit it. Didn't help that he found himself wondering more and more if she was right. But he had a plan, and he was going to stick to it. Be a long three years if he couldn't talk about his work with his best friend.

The high-pitched tones of small children filtered downstairs, even past the closed door, and each shriek of excitement sucked moisture from his mouth and spawned more butterflies in his stomach. Somehow, he'd thought the first fans he'd meet would be readers of the graphic novels he'd been working on for years. Not tiny children who seemed to love the cookie-cutter books he churned out.

He did his best to try to incorporate a message or somewhat advanced vocabulary so he didn't feel completely like he was pandering to Nectar's greed. His original idea had been badly corrupted by his boss and Nectar's marketing gurus, and he hadn't had the foresight to make sure it didn't happen. Now he was stuck with it, having invented Doctor Chicken and now acting as Nectar's despicable shill.

He checked the clock, smoothed the front of his shirt, and grabbed up a handful of slender picture books consisting of his most popular Doctor Chicken titles.

It could be worse. Gonzalez might have made him wear an actual chicken costume. With a bow tie.

AFTER the reading was finished, Stratford breathed a little easier. The kidlets had been incredibly attentive and certainly hadn't progressed to the age of heckling, but he'd found focusing on any one face was enough pressure to cause him to stumble in his fake, super-happy

Doctor Chicken persona. He'd intentionally blurred his vision so he didn't see the expression on any kid's face, and he sure as shit didn't look at any of the parents.

After half an hour reading, during which none of the parents denounced him as a complete fraud, the store manager had announced Doctor Chicken would be available to sign autographs for the next hour, and there were additional copies of Doctor Chicken books for sale. The thing that amazed him most was that four-year-old kids even cared about or understood autographs.

Since the cash registers had been ringing almost non-stop during his reading, Stratford assumed he'd be signing books for more than an hour. He was right. He'd been there for almost two hours, and his hand had gone past cramping into completely numb. Would signing until his stitches split qualify for Workman's Compensation?

He'd folded himself into a kiddie chair and tucked himself underneath what had to be a repurposed kindergarten craft table, and plastered on a big fake smile. Presumably he wasn't allowed to sit at a grown-up table, in a grown-up chair, because some marketing genius decided he shouldn't loom over the kids. When he made his own bookings and arranged for his own setup, he'd make some changes. There had to be a way to deal with this so he didn't end up broken and in spasm by the end of a torture session like this.

The bouncing excited kids were cute, for sure, but Stratford was glad their parents moved them along before he had to try to say much beyond asking them what their favorite character was. Usually it was the character featured in whatever book they had clutched in their tiny hands. A couple of them had even rounded the table to hug or kiss him. Too cute, but not cute enough that he was ever going to enjoy public appearances.

Finally, the last kid was before him. She was super cute, with big dark-brown eyes, long wavy hair that was almost black but not quite, and pale skin that reminded him of someone. Then he shook himself. He was simply punchy from the exhausting afternoon, and he wanted nothing more than to scuttle back to his apartment, order a pizza, and hide, giving the dead piece of meat at the end of his right elbow a chance to recover. Actually, he'd have to decide between a cab home and pizza for dinner. He wouldn't be able to afford both, not with both rent and electricity coming due at the end of the month.

The little girl was holding two books.

"Hi there, sweetie. What's your name?" Most of the kids were able to tell him their names, but if he didn't already know how to spell whatever they said, neither did the kids.

"Sienna."

"Sienna. That's a pretty name." As an artist at heart, Stratford was good with the color names; he wasn't going to need parental assistance with that one.

He reached out for her books. Sienna handed him one that was well loved. Gonzalez might hate that little Sienna's parents hadn't bought a brand-new book for him to sign, but Stratford didn't care. If he'd been allowed to guide the Doctor Chicken books in the way he wanted to, he might not hate his Doctor Chicken persona so much.

After signing his newly created, loopy Doctor Chicken signature, arm shaking with fatigue, he held a hand out for Sienna's second book and his very last autograph of the day.

"This one is for my uncle. He made me wait until the end. I don't know why."

Stratford was too tired to interpret the explanation. At this point, nothing mattered more than signing his pseudonym one last time. "Okay, sweetie. What's your uncle's name?"

"Vinnie."

Stratford had opened the brand-new book and readied the pen before his brain processed the name. Lifting his head, it didn't take long to lay eyes on Vinnie, standing by the door, arms crossed over his chest, looking both gorgeous and disapproving.

He wasn't sure if it was the success of standing up to Barry the previous night or his incredible numbing exhaustion, but the urge to run and hide was light-years behind the urge to let Vinnie take him home. Maybe Vinnie would wrap him in those strong arms that made everything better. He didn't need a knight in shining armor to save him, but maybe a sexy Italian knight to stand next to him and prop him up might be just the thing.

First, he had to erase that disapproval from Vinnie's face.

He grinned and shrugged, then winced when the movement pulled on the muscles clenched in their death throes.

Vinnie walked over to the table, looming over Stratford from his rather low vantage point.

"C'mon, *Doctor Chicken*. Let me drop Sienna off, and then I'll take you home. I think we maybe have some things to discuss."

Stratford shivered. That sounded ominous. Especially with the heavy emphasis on his pen name. But he wasn't going to bury his head in the sand with Vinnie, and the promise of a ride home didn't have anything to do with it.

"Okay."

"Uncle Vinnie, we're taking Doctor Chicken home with us?" Sienna was practically bouncing, her energy and enthusiasm positively draining to watch.

"No, honey, I'm taking you home, then I'm taking Doctor Chicken to his home."

"Oh." Sienna turned sad doe eyes on her uncle before she fizzled out.

"You got a bag or something?" Vinnie asked.

"Downstairs, in the employee lounge." It seemed so far away.

"Get your bag, Doctor," Vinnie ordered.

Stratford tried to comply. But his legs didn't have enough leverage to hoist himself out of the chair. Pushing his palms down on the tabletop was also a mistake, and he hissed in pain as his cramped, aching arm and still-healing wound flared to vicious life.

Without warning, Vinnie was there, the disapproval turned to concern. Slipping his hands under Stratford's shoulders, Vinnie lifted. For a moment, Stratford feared the small chair would forever be attached to his ass, but it shook free and clattered to the ground.

"Excuse me." Vinnie waved at the store manager, who had tried to look too busy to help, despite not actually doing anything at all. Vinnie, though, was a customer, not a fellow employee like Stratford, and his tone wasn't one to be ignored.

"Get Doctor Chicken's bag. He's leaving now."

"But the chairs...."

Vinnie growled. "You've got other employees who can do that, but I'm guessing Doctor Chicken has other appearances, and he's already been signing for hours with stitches in his hand. You don't want to be the reason he can't make it to those appearances, do you?"

The store manager—Greg, his nametag proclaimed—shook his head frantically.

"Good." Vinnie's glare hadn't lessened one bit. "Get his bag. We're leaving now."

Within moments, they were on their way. Sienna's excited burbling, which thankfully required very little response from either of them, filled the car, absolving him from trying to find any conversational topics. When they finally pulled up in front of a well-kept home not too far from his apartment, a vivacious, dark-haired beauty who looked a lot like Vinnie opened the door. Sienna ran to her as soon as Vinnie had disengaged all the appropriate buckles and whatnot. Stratford hunched down in his seat, trying to stay out of sight.

"I'll be back in a few minutes. You want to sit tight or you want come in?"

"I'll stay here, please." He didn't have the energy to make polite conversation. Feeling had begun returning to his hand, and it was pissed right-the-fuck off. Stratford thought he might spend the rest of the drive home clenching his teeth against a scream.

Vinnie spoke to his sister for a moment, then the three of them went inside. For the first time that day, Stratford was able to breathe. He knew it was only a momentary reprieve, because Vinnie wanted to "talk," which Stratford assumed meant Vinnie would yell at him for lying or mock him for being Doctor Chicken before telling him they shouldn't see each other anymore. Stratford hadn't had very many relationships, but after a few weird hours at class and one promising, spectacular date with Vinnie, he suspected Vinnie would hurt the most to lose.

Stratford didn't know how long he'd waited in the car. Didn't seem like long, even with the vicious pulses of agony in his hand, before Vinnie returned carrying a small bag.

As they started driving, Stratford sighed and rested his forehead against the cool glass of the window. He'd be the first to admit he entered every date hoping to find the one, dreaming of a future with guys he barely knew. He'd done it so often, that little burst of anticipation and hope was more than familiar. He didn't believe in love at first sight, but Vinnie was different than every other man he'd been involved with, and it scared the shit out of him that the difference meant he was about to lose the guy made for him.

The rest of the drive continued in silence, and if that put off the inevitable until Stratford was in the comfort of his own home, he wasn't going to be the one to open Vinnie's floodgates.

VINNIE kept glancing over at his passenger. Stratford had been great with those kids, and Vinnie hadn't been able to take his eyes off Stratford from the beginning of the reading. With every animated word Stratford spoke, and every minute Stratford had pretended not to see Vinnie, his anger grew. He'd wanted to wade through the throng of kids, pick Stratford up and shake him before kissing the stuffing out of him. It hadn't taken long for him to realize Stratford wasn't actually seeing anyone, and the periodic flashes of pain and panic in Stratford's eyes washed away Vinnie's anger.

The anger had returned, stronger than ever, while he watched Stratford sign. And sign. Then sign some more, well past the posted ending time. The store manager had stood there like a proud peacock, almost with dollar signs in his eyes like in one of Sienna's cartoon characters. Greg the manager didn't seem to notice or care that Stratford had stitches in his palm and was given an absolutely ridiculous chair and table to sit in. It wasn't as though kids Sienna's age never had to approach adults sitting in adult-sized chairs. This time, though, Vinnie's fury wasn't directed toward Stratford, although he wanted to know why Stratford hadn't mentioned this aspect of his work. Even Vinnie could admire the brilliant simplicity in Doctor Chicken's books. It was no surprise Sienna was hooked.

Just one more mystery to unwrap with that sexy little bow tie. Which wouldn't be tonight, unfortunately. Not with Stratford curled up on himself and cradling his right arm as though it would shatter into a million pieces. At least he knew Stratford hadn't been blowing him off yesterday when he'd said he wanted to see how he felt after his work event. It was too soon to expect Stratford to have called him and asked for help, and he doubted Stratford was going to easily recuperate without assistance. He sure as hell didn't want Stratford calling anyone else for help.

As if on cue, a muted ring sounded from Stratford's pocket. He struggled, wincing as he did so.

"Just let it go to voice mail."

"I can't. I'm sure it's my friend Abby, and she'll keep calling until she gets an answer."

Even though they were only a couple of blocks from Stratford's apartment, Vinnie pulled into the next driveway, threw the car into park, and pulled Stratford's phone out his pocket. Sadly, this time, he couldn't go fishing in Stratford's pants; the phone was in a jacket pocket. Vinnie handed the phone off and pulled back out into traffic.

"Hey, Abby."

Stratford paused a moment to listen and let out a weary chuckle. "No. No explosions or freak-outs. It just went longer than expected and I'm exhausted."

This time, Vinnie heard a murmur of a woman's voice but couldn't decipher any words.

"No thanks, Abby. I'm too tired. I'll call you later."

Stratford made his goodbyes and clicked off his phone as Vinnie parked outside his building. Before Stratford had his seatbelt unbuckled, Vinnie was around the other side of the car, opening the passenger door, like déjà vu.

While Stratford trudged to his door, Vinnie retrieved his bag and, this time, followed Stratford upstairs into his apartment.

They passed two doors in a short hallway before Stratford came to another one. The lock downstairs was a solid deadbolt, but the lock on this one was a little flimsy.

"You should talk to your landlord about changing the locks. This isn't safe, especially if your neighbors have guests who aren't reputable."

Stratford threw him an incredulous glance over his shoulder before fitting his key into the lock. "I don't have any neighbors. The other two doors are storage rooms for the clinic downstairs."

Vinnie wasn't sure if that made him feel better or worse. With no one around, what if Stratford got into trouble? He'd be completely on his own.

He forgot about his worries when the door to Stratford's apartment opened. He'd spent a lot of time wondering what it looked like, and now he was going to find out.

Following Stratford into a narrow hallway, he let the door close behind him. Turning for a second, he locked the door, then turned back just as Stratford grunted and stumbled.

"Okay, Bob, give me a minute."

Bob?

Stratford slung his bag on the floor and Vinnie saw the furry lump twining itself around Stratford's legs. He grinned. A cat. He and his mother had been too busy and too broke to get his sisters a pet, but Vinnie had always wanted a cat.

"You named your cat Bob?"

Stratford stepped into what could loosely be called a kitchen and flicked on the light switch. It had a tiny Formica table with two very old-fashioned vinyl-covered chairs. The one wall had the smallest fridge he'd ever seen, barely bigger than a bar fridge, a scuffed white counter with a single stainless-steel sink, a two-burner hot plate, and six cupboards, three below the counter and three on the wall above.

"His name's actually Bob Marley, but that's too long to say all the time. Have a seat. Bob will settle once I've fed him."

"No, you sit. Tell me what to do, and I'll feed him." Vinnie steered Stratford to a chair and pushed on his shoulders to make him sit. If Stratford hadn't been so sore, he probably would have fought Vinnie, but he settled in with a sigh.

The cat immediately transferred its attention to his legs, purring like crazy. What was that called again? Loving the one that fed you. Cupboard love? Something like that. His mom probably had some old-world expression for it, but Vinnie hadn't paid much attention when growing up, and after his dad died, he wasn't at home enough. He barely spoke any Italian, much to the chagrin of his grandmother, who still lived in Italy.

Stratford gave him his instructions, and Vinnie got to work. "So, Bob Marley? I take it you're a reggae fan."

Which he'd never have guessed, but then, musical tastes always surprised him.

"No, not really."

Vinnie put the rest of the can in the fridge and set Bob's dish down on the floor beside his water dish.

"Smoking up?" Vinnie's eyebrow rose. With so many years raising his younger sisters, he didn't much approve of drug use, but regular marijuana use should have made Stratford less skittish.

"No, never, actually."

Huh. A wince as Stratford shifted reminded Vinnie of his priorities.

"Come on. Let's get you in a nice warm shower. Loosen up those muscles a bit."

Stratford stared up at him, confused and lost. "What?"

"The hot water will help. Then I've got some lotion to rub in. Believe me, after the amount of time I've spent under cars or bending into them, I'm well acquainted with working the knots out of muscles."

Drawing in a deep stuttering breath, Stratford's eyes got red and shiny. "Aren't you dumping me?"

The words practically cut Vinnie off at the knees. He dropped down in front of Stratford. "Why would you think that?"

"You said we had to talk."

Vinnie kissed the tip of Stratford's long, pointed nose. "Sometimes, that just means I want some more information, you know? And it's information that can wait until you're not in so much pain. This maybe isn't what I'd had in mind for a third date, but I'm really glad I was at that Nectar store because I want to be able to help you. We're going to work on your arm a little and order in some dinner."

Standing, Vinnie pretended not to notice Stratford dipping his head and wiping at his face. At some point, Stratford would learn he didn't have to hide his upset from him, but it was early days yet.

Vinnie helped Stratford to his feet, the man still stiff from being crumpled into a pretzel for the better part of three hours.

The bathroom wasn't hard to find in the tiny apartment, and bag in hand, Vinnie followed Stratford's shuffling gait.

"So why Bob Marley, then?"

Vinnie latched on to anything to distract himself from the bow tie he was undoing, slowly, the way he'd like to before throwing Stratford on a bed. His cock took notice, but Vinnie ignored it as best he could.

"You're going to think I'm an idiot."

"Of course I won't." Vinnie hung the bow tie over a towel rack and bit his lip before starting to undo Stratford's shirt buttons. They'd fumbled for a bit before it became clear that Stratford's fingers weren't up to the fine motor coordination required, but Vinnie couldn't convince his body he wasn't stripping Stratford for his cock's approval. This really wasn't how he wanted to see Stratford naked for the first time.

"Bob is actually my boyfriend's cat."

Vinnie tensed, and Stratford corrected himself. "Ex-boyfriend's, I mean. We hadn't been together for very long, but six months ago, he asked me to take care of Bob for him. I said yes, only to find out that he meant forever, while he moved to the west coast with his *other* boyfriend. The one who was allergic to cats."

"That's, that's...."

"Yeah, we weren't really a good fit. I sometimes wonder if he only dated me because he needed a sucker to take the cat before he moved."

"Well, I think the only idiot in this story is him. And even if finding Bob a home was why he dated you, Bob's lucky to have you."

"He's definitely grown on me."

Vinnie peeled back Stratford's shirt, clenching his fists in the fabric for a moment to keep from tracing the light muscle definition visible on Stratford's flat stomach. His small, coppery nipples had drawn up in the chill of the room, or so Vinnie sternly told himself. Nothing to do with sexual tension.

"I assume you haven't taken Bob to the vet yet."

"Uh, no. Nik left his vaccination schedule tucked in the carrier. I suppose that should have been a dead giveaway. But he's not due for a few more months."

"You might want to get Bob sexed while you're there." Vinnie had reached Stratford's belt, and it took every ounce of concentration and willpower to continue with the conversation and stay focused on the task at hand, rather than stroke a fingertip along the twitching length clearly visible beneath Stratford's fly.

"Why do you say that?" Stratford sounded as breathless as Vinnie felt.

"Because that black-and-orange coloring is sex-linked. Usually only females have it." The zipper's teeth releasing made sweat pop out on Vinnie's neck.

"How do you know that?"

"I read a lot." And he did. Not a lot of fiction, but he read a lot of articles, newspapers, and non-fiction. His lack of formal education bothered him sometimes, and the solution to that was to educate himself as best he could. He didn't want it to be obvious he'd never been to college.

Pressing his lips together, Vinnie grabbed the waistband of Stratford's pants and boxer briefs, yanking them down in one swift move before he sprang away and stood up. Naked, Stratford was everything Vinnie could want. Lanky and strong, with smooth, pale skin. Brown hair scattered lightly between his nipples, fading over his belly and darkening again below his navel in a path leading directly to a neatly trimmed bush. Stratford's cock, long, thin, and pink, stood proudly from his groin, and it was all Vinnie could do to keep from kneeling again and opening his mouth. He also took note of the bruises on both knees along with an angry-looking scab, presumably from the tumble Stratford took outside the community center.

"Guess I'll have to start calling her Marley, then."

When Stratford made a move to cover his groin with his hands, Vinnie forced his gaze upward. Stratford's cheeks were pink, and Vinnie could kick his own ass for making Stratford uncomfortable. Despite Stratford's physical reaction, Vinnie was here to help him, not ravish him.

Vinnie cleared his throat and started the water running. "Marley's a good name. She friendly when she's not getting fed?"

"Yeah, absolutely. He's... I mean, she's heavy, but she likes to lay on your chest and is perfectly happy to be carried around. I don't often have people in my apartment." Stratford gave a little negligent shrug. "But when I have, she's happy with whatever attention she can get."

Vinnie tested the water. At least Stratford could get hot water and fairly quick. He opened his bag, which held the personal first-aid kit he'd compiled after years of dealing with a handful of girls who threw themselves headlong into everything, and pulled out a latex glove. Careful not to risk another glance at Stratford's cock, he slid the glove over Stratford's dressing and secured it with surgical tape. At this point, the stitches would normally be okay to get wet, but he was concerned the hours of signing might have opened the wound a bit, and he wanted the chance to clean it and dress it properly.

He helped Stratford into the shower and positioned him slightly bent over so the spray landed on his upper back and ran down his arms.

"Stay like that for a bit, try to relax. Are you okay if I find you something clean to wear?"

"Uh-huh." From Stratford's almost sensual tone, Vinnie knew the hot water was starting to work.

"Okay, I'll be back." He grabbed his bag and took it with him.

As with the bathroom, it wasn't hard to find the bedroom. There wasn't a living room or den or office. Just a bedroom. Stratford had done his best with the confined space and managed to fit a dresser, desk, bed, and a couple of chairs and bookshelves in the room. A TV and DVD player sat on the dresser, across from the bed.

By far, the most eye-catching feature of the room was the pages and pages of hand drawn characters tacked up on the wall. The layout was as haphazard as Sienna's drawings on the playroom walls, but these drawings were incredible. Despite the exaggerated proportions of the characters, which seemed to be superheroes, although Vinnie didn't recognize any of them, they were so life-like, ready to leap of the page and take action. Few of them were colored, most of them done in black or blue ink.

Where had Stratford gotten all of those?

Then Vinnie noticed the sketchpads and drawing utensils on the desk beside a laptop. He should have known when Stratford had told him he did graphic design. He flipped through the book and confirmed his suspicions. A few of the pages had distinctly different characters, characters that were clearly destined for Doctor Chicken books. Why hadn't Stratford told him about any of this? There had been ample opportunity to do so when they'd had dinner, but Vinnie realized now Stratford had been deftly avoiding talking about his work and exactly what he did. Much like Vinnie had, although it hadn't been hard to draw on his early days in the shop for stories.

Vinnie wanted—needed—to know more about this. He closed the sketchbook and hovered by Stratford's nightstand. There was no good reason to suppose Stratford kept his underwear in there, but he couldn't quite control his curiosity.

A battered bottle of lube and a partial box of condoms lay amongst the TV and DVD remotes, as well as a few DVD cases. None of them were porn, though, and no dildos or vibrators or nipple clamps. There was zero information about Stratford's likes in that drawer. He wasn't even sure if Stratford was a top, bottom, or switch, although Vinnie sort of despised those labels. The bed looked comfortable, sporting a plain headboard with basic wooden slats. Unmade, of course, but Vinnie didn't expect anything else. If he didn't live with his mom, who insisted on made beds, he'd probably never make his own. What was the point, really?

Flipping the covers back, he smoothed out the sheet underneath. He placed a few bottles on the dresser, then shoved the bag against the wall. It would be more relaxing for Stratford if he redressed his wound in here. Next on the agenda was a massage to release the tension in those cramped arms.

He shook himself and closed the drawer before heading to the dresser. The first drawer on the top he opened held a mishmash of boxer briefs in assorted colors. He pulled out a pair of forest-green ones that would look great against Stratford's skin.

Taking one last look around the room, and remembering the tiny kitchen, the lack of car, he wondered about Stratford's lifestyle. Those Doctor Chicken books were incredibly popular, and now it was even more than the books. Greeting cards, stuffed animals, ornaments, stickers, and a forthcoming online game geared to young kids. Stratford must be very frugal or saving for something spectacular, because he had to be pulling in more than Vinnie was. Even after sending one sister through an MBA program, another in undergrad, and the third poised to begin, Vinnie wasn't exactly hurting. Stratford might not need a lot of extra room, but it would only be a couple hundred more a month to pay for an apartment with a proper kitchen. Why hadn't Stratford bothered?

More mysteries Vinnie wanted answers for, answers he wasn't going to get tonight. Not if he had his way. Stratford was getting patched up, massaged, fed, and then put to bed. Probably alone, if Vinnie could make himself leave. Even without the prospect of sex, Vinnie wanted to curl around that long body, warming it.

Mindful of how long he'd left Stratford in the shower, he pulled out his phone and dialed home.

"Hey, Mama. I might not be home tonight."

Although he rarely spent a night away from home—for personal reasons—his mother had long accepted that he was an adult entitled to his own life. In fact, she'd been pushing him for the past few years to find a boyfriend, telling him it was his turn to make a life that wasn't simply taking care of her and his sisters. After telling him to be careful and that she wanted to meet Stratford if it was serious, she hung up.

He tucked his phone away and went to retrieve Stratford.

Seven

VINNIE stood at the foot of Stratford's bed, unable to do more than stare at the sleek body stretched out face down before him. For his own sanity and to assist his crumbling self-control, he'd put Stratford in a pair of boxer briefs after drying him off. Stratford's erection had shown signs of returning, but he got Stratford's privates covered up and him face down on the bed before either of them got carried away.

Cleaning and rebandaging Stratford's hand hadn't been fraught with sexual temptation, but now Vinnie was going to lay hands on Stratford's skin. If it weren't for the boxer briefs, Vinnie would lay odds that Stratford's massage would start with Vinnie's face buried between those round buttocks. Wasn't supposed to be that sort of massage. Nevertheless, Vinnie stripped down to his own briefs. The massage oil he'd brought would completely ruin his clothes, and he'd swear to that on a stack of Bibles. As long as he was careful to keep his erection—already straining at his y-fronts—away from Stratford's body, he could keep this clinical.

He poured a small amount of oil in his palms and rubbed them together to warm the oil. Picking up Stratford's right arm, he began massaging Stratford's arm and fingers. He'd work his way up the arm before working on the rest of Stratford's back, because he suspected the arm might need some more attention after he'd gotten the rest of Stratford's upper body relaxed.

The minutes passed by quickly as Vinnie was hypnotized by both the even strokes of his hands over Stratford's skin and the low, guttural moans of a well-pleased man. He couldn't help but assume Stratford might make those same sounds during sex—the explosion in the car had happened so fast, Vinnie didn't have enough time to catalog or retain Stratford's sex noises.

Vinnie moved his hands down to Stratford's lower back, and Stratford started writhing. Vinnie swallowed a groan. This was hard enough without Stratford moving. Stratford's ass started lifting, as though asking for something Vinnie hadn't planned to give tonight.

"Stop that." He swatted those round globes, and Stratford sucked in a breath before he pressed his hips up further, drawing his arms back as though he was going to get up on all fours.

Vinnie stretched out to stop him, nestling his own leaking cock right in the dip of Stratford's lower back. Two thin layers of cotton between them was almost nothing.

They both groaned in unison, and Vinnie couldn't prevent himself from bucking a couple of times against Stratford.

"Please, Vinnie, please."

"Your hands and arms need to rest." Vinnie's voice, pitched low from his almost overwhelming arousal, didn't sound like him at all.

"I don't care," Stratford pleaded, as desperate as Vinnie felt. "I want you." He shimmied against Vinnie, putting more pressure on a cock that was just about ready to blow just from massaging Stratford's goddamned back.

Stratford's attempt to move his hand underneath him, presumably to jack himself off, snapped most of Vinnie's control. He wasn't going to risk hurting Stratford, but they both wanted and needed to get off.

He flipped Stratford onto his back.

STRATFORD stared up at Vinnie, hardly able to believe he'd managed to convince Vinnie to have sex. Hell, he was surprised Vinnie was here at all. Being taken care of had been… amazing and wonderful, and it had been… well, no man had ever been so focused on his comfort. But the massage had gradually shifted from pain release and muscle relaxation to a sensual torture Stratford wasn't sure he'd survive.

The brief brushes of Vinnie's hard-on against his back told him Vinnie had to be holding back for his sake, not because Vinnie didn't want him. And he was ready to fucking explode. He wanted them to be together like they had been in the car. He wanted to see what Vinnie looked like naked and aroused. He wanted to taste Vinnie's salty skin and feel the texture of the precum wetting the front of Vinnie's briefs.

Vinnie's eyes were dilated, his dark hair wild and his body... gorgeous. Stratford pumped his hips involuntarily. Solid biceps and mouthwatering broad shoulders framed firm pecs covered in a mat of dark hair leading down to a belly that... didn't have a six-pack. In fact, Vinnie's belly was smooth, a little soft, and Stratford found that even sexier. He knew he was scrawny compared to Vinnie, but seeing that Vinnie was sexy and gorgeous but not perfect made him all the more comfortable.

In fact, Vinnie looked as fierce as a warrior, intent on plundering Stratford's body. He stripped off the boxer briefs with reckless haste—so unlike the careful way he'd covered Stratford after his shower earlier.

Completely exposed, with Vinnie between his legs, Stratford expected a demand for condoms and lube. He'd already stretched an arm out to his nightstand to show Vinnie where they were when Vinnie dove down and sucked his cock down almost all the way to his pubes.

Stratford let out a drawn-out moan and twined his fingers in the sheets to keep from thrusting all the way down Vinnie's throat. His cock wasn't wide, but it was long, and he didn't want to choke the man who, in two seconds, was giving him better head than Barry had managed after ten minutes. Vinnie's tongue was everywhere and not a tooth graze to be had. Like the previous night, Stratford found himself ready to blow way too soon, although the massage might be considered an hour of foreplay.

"Vinnie, Vinnie." He didn't know if he was asking Vinnie to stop or to keep going. He stared down his body, and Vinnie looked back at him.

Those brown eyes were almost black, and Stratford hadn't realized how fabulous those pink lips would look around his dick. Somehow, he hadn't even pictured Vinnie as a guy who'd like sucking anyone off, but as the suction increased, Stratford gasped, so damn glad Vinnie was that type of guy.

"Vinnie, I'm gonna...."

In response, Vinnie lifted his head, leaving Stratford's cock in the open, spit-slick and waving in the breeze. His nostrils flared, because, for the first time in his life, he wanted to grab a guy's head and jam his mouth over his dick, let himself fuck into a warm, willing mouth. But he wasn't willing to be that aggressive with Vinnie. Not when this had already grown into something more than just sex.

With glittering eyes, Vinnie peered at him. He only had a second to wonder if he looked as desperate and horny before Vinnie bent back to engulf his cock. This time he only sucked half of it into his mouth, but urged Stratford to place his uninjured left hand on Vinnie's head. With his hand heavy atop Stratford's, he bobbed a bit.

Stratford tried a few shallow thrusts, not sure how Vinnie had read the desire in his eyes. Vinnie's gaze flicked up and caught his. All Stratford could see in those dark depths was an invitation.

Firmly, but not too fast, he pulled Vinnie's face down. Vinnie swallowed him all the way down, lips grazing the hair at his groin. He pulled Vinnie's head back, just a bit, then held him still as he fucked up into Vinnie's welcoming mouth.

Oh God. This was the best head he'd ever had. Saliva trailed down his cock, wetting his pubes, and the sucking sounds combined with Vinnie's ability and desire to take him all the way down destroyed any chance Stratford could stretch out the experience.

"Vinnie." The only other sound he was able to get out was a strangled shout as he poured himself down Vinnie's throat while his heart slammed against his ribs and his body twisted as though he'd been electrocuted.

Vinnie held him in his mouth until he stopped pulsating. Stratford relaxed back on the bed, ready to return the favor as soon as he got his breath back, but Vinnie, still frenzied, rose over Stratford's body and kissed him while resting his weight entirely on one arm.

This was the plundering Stratford had expected, although the appendages were slightly different. Vinnie's tongue had the bitter aftertaste of Stratford's cum, which Stratford chased after with his own tongue. Vinnie's bare cock—and Stratford hadn't noticed when Vinnie had removed his own briefs—lay hot and hard against his belly for a brief moment before Vinnie took himself in hand.

There wasn't so much as a brief break in the kiss, but Vinnie's tongue fucked his mouth as vigorously as he imagined Vinnie would plow his body when they got to that point. Stratford couldn't bear not to touch, and he wrapped a hand above Vinnie's to cover the slick, domed head of Vinnie's cock.

Vinnie fed a groan into his mouth and spurted all over their hands, painting Stratford's belly. His lips stilled while he shook, and he pulled his head back to gulp a few breaths before he twisted to the side and collapsed on the bed.

The gentle fingers stroking along his arm woke Stratford from the daze of a fantastic orgasm. Turning on his side, he inspected the man who'd now given him two incredible orgasms and hadn't said one word about them not being "real" because nobody had had anal sex. Stratford didn't have anything against anal sex, and based on Vinnie's explorations the previous night in the car, he didn't object to it, either, but Stratford resented, just a bit, the implication that sex required anal penetration.

Vinnie smiled at him, relaxed and sated. Stratford smiled back, more than ready to believe Vinnie's assertion that "we need to talk" in this case meant exactly what it said, without any ominous overtones. Then Stratford's stomach growled as though he hadn't eaten in... a day. He'd been too nervous to eat before his reading, so dinner the previous night had been the last time.

Laughing, Vinnie reached over and rubbed his belly, heedless of the cum cooling there. "Let's get you cleaned up and fed. I'm supposed to do that before I jump your bones, aren't I?"

Just the fact that Vinnie wasn't planning to exit immediately after climaxing was impressive enough, never mind everything he'd done for Stratford.

Placing his hand over Vinnie's, he waited until Vinnie met his gaze. "Thank you. I really appreciate it."

Stretching his neck out, Vinnie placed a gentle kiss on his lips. "I know we haven't known each other long, but please believe me. I did it for me as much as you. All I want is for you to be safe and happy."

Stratford wanted to believe him. He had a bad habit of jumping into relationships with both feet, going to dates expecting the sun and moon and getting the ass end of a troll. This time, though, it felt like he'd gotten the sun, moon, and a bonus unicorn. He sent out a little prayer to the universe that this was the man he'd spent his whole life searching for... and if so, not to let him fuck it up.

Vinnie bounded out of bed and brought back a damp towel from the bathroom. He wiped them both up and grabbed their underwear from where he'd tossed it on the floor.

"You've got a lot of energy." Stratford wasn't even sure he'd be able to stay awake long enough to eat, even though he didn't want to miss a moment of Vinnie hanging out in his apartment.

He shrugged. "Sex does that to me. Besides, I'm also not the one starving to death. Pizza okay, or did you want Chinese?" Vinnie had taken his smartphone out of his pants pocket but let the pants drop to the floor again.

"Pizza's fine. Anything but anchovies."

Vinnie nodded and tapped out a few keys. Stratford had a momentary spurt of jealousy. He had a smartphone too, but a much older, refurbished model. He couldn't get a lot of the delivery apps to work on it, not that he could afford delivery too often. Most times, dinner was some sort of sandwich or soup unless Abby was feeding him or he was out on a date. He tried to remember if he had any money squirreled away in his emergency stash that he could contribute to dinner. Sitting up caught Vinnie's attention.

"Where are you going?"

"I was going to grab some money."

"Nuh-uh. Already paid for. C'mon." Vinnie jumped back into bed and wrestled him back. Laughing, Stratford let Vinnie press their bodies together.

"So...." Vinnie drawled out the word, but Stratford had no idea what he was leading up to.

"So?"

"Why didn't you tell me you were the very famous and popular Doctor Chicken?"

A wave of heated embarrassment swept him from head to toe. "Oh. That. I'm not famous."

"You are joking, right? I thought my niece was going to lose her fucking mind when she found out she was going to meet you. Considering how much I've spent for Doctor Chicken merchandise, I ought to do every parent in the world a favor and keep you too occupied to come up with new stories. It's going to get ten times worse once they get that website online."

Stratford shuddered, imagining Gonzalez's reaction if he slowed production.

Frowning, Vinnie traced a finger along his jaw, the rasping and light touch making Stratford shiver. If he could get it up this soon after blowing, his cock would be asking for seconds. Vinnie was great with his hands, but Vinnie's uncertain expression told Stratford he wasn't thinking about sex. Not this second, at any rate.

"I don't know how to ask this without sounding… hung up on money. I mean, I do okay, so don't think that. But how come you live here? I'm not joking, that Doctor Chicken stuff is like kiddie crack. I don't know how you do it, except I was able to tell right away that you were smart. And clearly talented."

Vinnie waved a hand at Stratford's sketches plastered on the wall. He supposed it made his room look a bit like a teenager's, but seeing bits of his dream everyday helped get him through the grueling, soul-crushing job at Nectar. Which, riding on the crest of the best sex of his life, he did not want to discuss. Talking work would only ruin what had turned into a really great day.

"You like them?" Vinnie didn't need to blow smoke up his ass, not now.

"Are you kidding? I'm sure you could do as well with those as you do with Doctor Chicken. A different demographic, obviously."

Stratford snorted at the dryly sarcastic statement. "No kidding."

"You didn't answer my question." Vinnie held his chin still, forcing Stratford to meet his gaze. "No hiding."

Wow. It hadn't taken Vinnie long to zero in on his modus operandi, Stratford's natural state of avoidance. Most people didn't care enough to even notice when Stratford managed to steer a conversation away from himself or things that made him uncomfortable.

"You turned a shitty, shitty day into something good. Something awesome, in fact. Talking about my job will destroy all that. Can we not do it?"

Vinnie thought about that for a moment before nodding. "Okay. But know that it's not forgotten. Especially because I can see it's something that upsets you. Sharing it might just make it better or easier to deal with. Think about that, okay?"

"Sure."

Vinnie smiled and gave him another kiss. "I guess I ought to put some pants on. Don't necessarily want to give the pizza guy a free show of the goods." He leapt out of bed and swung his hips in a mocking imitation of a stripper, dispelling the heavy tension that had threatened to annihilate Stratford's good mood.

Stratford checked the time and considered the tenderness Vinnie had displayed. "I don't know how much longer I'll be awake, but maybe you might want to call your mom?"

He'd never asked anyone to stay the night before. It had happened, sure, with previous boyfriends who'd fallen asleep after sex, but he'd never consciously wanted someone to spend the night in his bed, not when he was 99 percent sure they'd just be sleeping.

Surprisingly, Vinnie looked embarrassed. "Uh, I already called her. Told her I probably wouldn't be home."

"When?"

"While you were in the shower."

"But you didn't even know I'd be up for sex at all then."

Vinnie got that pitying look on his face. "It didn't matter. It doesn't matter. I wanted to stay with you. That doesn't have to mean sex, you know. Never. If you don't feel up to it, don't ever think you need to 'let me' just so I'll stick around."

Not feel up to it. What the hell was Vinnie smoking? Stratford had begun to wonder if he'd permanently damaged his hand—scary, because that was his drawing hand—and Vinnie had been able to coax an erection out of him just by kneeling in the general direction of his crotch. Nevertheless, Vinnie seemed to be waiting for some sort of response, pants half on and half off, that intense expression on his face.

"I promise."

Those seemed to be the words Vinnie had been waiting for, because he pulled on his pants just in time for the buzzer to the downstairs door to ring.

STRATFORD squinted against the sandpaper insistently rubbing across his eyelid.

"Bob... I mean, Marley, let me sleep," Stratford whispered, trying to shove the enormous fur ball off the bed. Marley was a determined cat, though. At least Stratford was on his side, because her normal wake-up trick was to stick her sandpaper tongue up his nose.

He sneezed and shook his head. Nope, she managed to find a nostril just fine. "Off."

Having decided he was adequately awakened, she dropped to the floor with a solid, reverberating thud. Now that he was safe from sandpaper, Stratford blinked an eye open. An arm lay heavy across his body, the smell of pepperoni strong in his nostrils. He blinked again, but something red and indistinct was squished up against his cheek.

He didn't want to disturb Vinnie, not after having the most restful sleep he'd had in a long time, but the pepperoni smell was really strong. Pushing himself up, the object came into view. A piece of pizza with a couple of bite marks, sat on a plate, glaring reproachfully from the bed just below his pillow. Both sheets and pillow had a few smears of sauce, and he wiped at his face. Dried flakes of sauce decorated his cheek, and he scratched a little. Was that cheese?

Letting out a little squawk, Stratford sat all the way up, pushing Vinnie's arm off.

Vinnie's hand moved over his back. "Morning, babe."

"Um." Stratford froze, not sure how to hide this.

He didn't have a chance, because Vinnie stretched around to peer up at him. A low chuckle rumbled in Vinnie's chest as he swiped a finger along Stratford's cheek.

"You were so fucking tired last night, I was lucky to keep you awake for two slices. The third, you curled up around it, and you wouldn't let me move it. I was starting to wonder just how much you love pizza. Funniest thing I ever saw. I can't believe you didn't move the whole night."

That made two of them. Stratford didn't know what to say or do. Why the hell had Vinnie stayed when Stratford acted like such a goof?

Vinnie sat up, nuzzling his nose along Stratford's neck. "Mmm. You smell delicious. Better than cologne. But you may want to wash the grease out of your hair."

He plucked a pepperoni slice out of Stratford's hair and dropped it on the plate. The absurdity of him sleeping with a slice of pizza managed to outweigh his mortification at it, and a tiny chuckle escaped.

Vinnie kissed his spine, a few huffing chuckles chasing warm breath over Stratford's skin. "What did you want to do today?"

"Besides shower and wash my hair, you mean?"

"Yep. We could hang out in bed all day, or we could go... anywhere, really. The museum, planetarium, science center."

Stratford shivered. If he was dreaming, he didn't want to wake up. A full weekend date, including a daytime date without either or both of them nursing a hangover. This was what it was supposed to be all about.... Oh, shit.

"I can't." Stratford dropped his head into his hands, hardly able to believe he was refusing Vinnie.

Vinnie's kisses got more insistent, drawing Stratford's skin into his mouth, bringing gooseflesh up on Stratford's neck.

"Are you sure?"

Stratford hadn't noticed his morning wood when Marley had been trying to buff the inside of his nose to a new shine, but with Vinnie's husky rumble and lips hitting every sensitive spot on his back—spots he didn't even know he had—it was hard to remember why he couldn't spend the day letting Vinnie have his way.

"This sounds stupid, but it's laundry day today. I skipped last week, and I need to get to the Laundromat today. With the sheets, it could take all day." Not that Stratford had any objection to washing sheets when they'd been messed up in the best way possible, but he never had the energy for the Laundromat during the week, and on the weekend, he was never able to snag more than one of the machines. The closest and cheapest place also had the tiniest washers, but for the money he saved, he couldn't afford to be picky about how long it took.

"Uh-huh. Well, why don't you bring your laundry to my place?"

That seemed oddly intimate, even though they'd explored almost every inch of each other's skin with their mouths. There were a few inches Stratford was still dying to taste. Intimacy aside, there were several other significant reasons to shoot that idea down.

"What about your mother? Sisters? I'm not ready to meet them." Not until he had a better sense of where his relationship with Vinnie was going, and especially not when Vinnie's mom damn well knew where Vinnie had been last night.

"I know, but that's why it's perfect." Vinnie craned his neck to peer at Stratford's alarm clock. "They'll be leaving for church in about an hour. After, they all have plans. Gabriella and her boyfriend are taking Sienna to see Santa, Evie's studying at a friend's for midterms, Marissa and my mom are going to a bridal shower for one of Marissa's friends. We've got a huge washing machine and tons of uninterrupted time for you to use it."

"You don't have to go to see Santa with your family?"

"Nope. I've done it plenty, and taking Sienna to Doctor Chicken let me out of that. That Doctor Chicken guy? Is fucking hot. I got the best end of that deal."

Even the sweet compliment wasn't quite enough to break through Stratford's trepidation. Once again, Vinnie seemed too good to be true. "Let me get this straight. You want to spend part of your weekend at home while I do laundry."

"No. I want to spend time with you. And if you need to do laundry, then I'm offering a way we can do both."

Vinnie's hands had gotten into the game, one of them sliding slowly down Stratford's belly, clearly on a mission. When a firm grip wrapped around his already straining cock, the only thing Stratford knew was he didn't want to be apart from Vinnie today.

"Okay."

"Good," Vinnie purred into his ear. "Let's make sure your sheets are well and truly dirtied before we get you in the shower and maybe get you filthy all over again. Then we'll go to my place and do laundry."

When had doing laundry ever sounded so good?

Vinnie pulled him back into bed, shoved the pizza plate onto the floor, then proceeded to demonstrate that the previous night hadn't been a fluke; Vinnie truly had been gifted by the blowjob gods.

"FOR the love of God, Vinnie, you'd better be dressed." Marissa's voice was exasperated, and shrill enough to yank Vinnie out the heated daze Stratford had created with little more than kisses.

Stratford leapt out of his arms and stood in front of the couch, eyes darting around the room searching for an escape while he frantically rebuttoned his shirt, tucked it back into his pants, and zipped them up.

"Who is that?" The whisper sounded panicky, and Vinnie cursed whatever mishap had brought Marissa, and presumably his mother, home between church and the shower.

"My sister, Marissa." Maybe his mom would wait in the car.

"Vinnie, *mi caro*, are you home? I want to hear all about the boy that kept you out all night."

Nope, Mama wasn't waiting in the car.

Stratford mouthed "Boy?" even as his cheekbones reddened, in anger or embarrassment or both.

"And my mama. Everyone my age and younger are boys." Great. If this was the last way he wanted to introduce Stratford to his family, he could only imagine how stressed Stratford was right now. The weekend had been going so well—overall—up until now.

"Your mother?" If there had been any sibilants in that statement, Stratford would have hissed.

"Uh, yeah."

The surprise had chased away Stratford's erection, but the puffy lips, mussed hair, and wrongly buttoned shirt would tell anyone, especially a seasoned mother, just exactly what Vinnie and Stratford had been doing while waiting for Stratford's laundry. He'd been about to pull Stratford's cock out into the open before stripping off his shirt. Vinnie shrugged. The timing could have been worse.

Marissa and his mom walked into the room, his mom making a little sound of surprise. Now that Vinnie's own erection had deflated, he rose to stand beside Stratford.

"Mama, Marissa, this is Stratford. Stratford, my sister Marissa and my mom Gina."

"Well, aren't you an adorable boy." His mom threw him a triumphant grin before she rounded the couch to pinch Stratford's cheeks. Stratford stood still, like a possum who thought if he didn't move, the predator wouldn't find him. "It's so nice to meet you. Vinnie doesn't bring many boys home to meet his mama. You must be the infamous Doctor Chicken that my *bellissima* Sienna can't stop talking about."

Now Vinnie's cheeks heated. He was thirty-four, not fourteen. "Mama, what are you doing home?" Because that didn't sound guilty at all.

His mother shrugged. "I forgot to put the gift in the car when we went to church. What are you doing here?"

Marissa stood just behind their mother. She held up a pair of boxer briefs, a bright red pair, the waistband pinched between her thumb and index finger. "Yes, Vinnie, what are you doing here?"

His sister was only teasing, and probably had no idea they weren't even Vinnie's because how would she know he never wore boxer briefs, but Stratford wouldn't understand the way his sisters teased him. A flush so dark it almost looked unhealthy lit up Stratford's face, and with a strangled gasp, he leapt over the back of the couch, snatched the underwear out of Marissa's hands, and kept on going out the front door. Unlike most of the incidents Vinnie had witnessed, Stratford displayed an incredible grace.

The front door closed behind Stratford with a bang, leaving a startled silence in its wake.

"Fuck." The word slipped out, and his mother glared at him. He didn't fucking care that he was growling at his sister. "I swear to God,

Marissa, if you scared him away, you'll be working weekends until you're forty. I like this one."

Vinnie grabbed his wallet, jacket, and the coat Stratford had left behind in his panicked flight, in case he couldn't coax the man back inside, even to pick up his laundry.

"What? I was just teasing." Marissa sounded almost as bad as Evie complaining that life wasn't fair. "I didn't know Vinnie was in the habit of stripping out on the front lawn."

Vinnie kept his glare on, full strength. "I've known the man all of a week. He's nervous about meeting family—I suspect he was kicked out at an early age—and we came over here to do laundry so he didn't have to spend all day at the Laundromat." Each word became more distinct and louder until the last word was almost a shout.

Marissa blanched. "They're *his* underwear?"

"Marissa." His mother's voice was reproachful. Ha. His mom had forgotten all about his swearing transgression.

"Now, I'm going to go chase him down, because you'll notice he was so embarrassed he left without wearing a coat."

Marissa sputtered an apology, but Vinnie slammed the front door on it. He wasn't interested in her apology, only how far Stratford had managed to get in those few minutes.

On the porch, he scanned the street but couldn't see Stratford's hair anywhere. Damn, that guy could fucking fly. Vinnie's street was residential enough that he was almost 100 percent certain Stratford hadn't managed to grab a cab in less than five minutes.

Patting down the pockets of Stratford's jacket, he groaned. He couldn't even call because his phone was in Vinnie's grasp. "Fuck." Vinnie spoke low and glanced guiltily over his shoulder in case his mother had followed him out. He must have headed to the bus stop on the main street.

Slipping on his jacket, he walked down the driveway. If Stratford wasn't at the bus stop, he'd take out the car and start driving.

On the sidewalk he looked both ways as he tried to remember which street had the closest bus stop.

"Hey."

The quiet greeting had him whipping around. Stratford sat on the bumper of the Navigator, shoulders slumped, twisting the waistband of his underwear.

The minor adrenaline rush eased, and Vinnie wondered if he was going to have to get used to sprints like this or whether Stratford would eventually trust him enough not to bolt, or at least, not bolt away from him.

"Hey." Vinnie helped Stratford into his jacket and tipped Stratford's face back so they were looking at each other. "You okay?"

"Yeah, I'm sorry. I've never been caught by anyone's parents before, and I don't want your mom to hate me. Then there was my underwear, and, well… I panicked."

"It's okay. They don't hate you." Vinnie dropped a kiss on his lips. Putting himself out there too early maybe wasn't wise, but he was going take a chance in case that was what Stratford needed. "Look. It's not a secret that I want you to meet them. We haven't known each other long, but I'm hoping this is the first weekend together of many, many more. You'll soon see that my sisters might occasionally be pains in the ass, but they mean well. And my mother, well, she's thrilled I'm bringing someone home. She'll always see the good in people, and I think there's a lot of good in you to see."

This time the blush was faint but healthy. Stratford licked his lips, and after an invitation like that, Vinnie couldn't do anything but kiss him. Stratford returned it wholeheartedly… for a moment. Then he started pushing at Vinnie's shoulders.

For a split second, Vinnie freaked, but he relaxed again when he noticed Stratford's wide smile.

"Not while we could get caught again, okay?"

Vinnie nodded. "Will you come in and meet them for real? They really are only here for a few minutes. My mom forgot the shower gift. And I think my sister is more embarrassed by having picked up your underwear than you are. Then we can go back to enjoying the fire."

He'd lit one just for Stratford when he'd admired the fireplace, almost wistfully saying how much he loved them.

Stratford's blush flared up for a second. "I can't believe she touched my underwear. That's just awful."

Vinnie waggled his brows, snatched up the boxer briefs, and held them over his face, sniffing. "I don't think they're awful."

"Stop that." Stratford's words were almost lost in his laughter. He tried to smack Vinnie's shoulder and grab the cotton at the same time. "Hide those away somewhere. I'm not going back in there holding them."

"Okay, sure." Vinnie stuffed them in his pocket, accompanied by another eyebrow wiggle. Stratford's laugh eased a fear deep inside that he'd managed to break their fragile connection already.

Five more minutes and then he'd have Stratford to himself again.

Eight

JUST before noon, Stratford's desk phone rang. He hesitated, hand hovering over the receiver. Usually a call right before lunch meant some stupid, last-minute task that meant he'd be working through lunch again. If he left this very second, he could pretend he'd just missed the call. Gonzalez stepped out of his office, and Stratford snatched up the phone. If Gonzalez wanted to talk to him, maybe the phone would divert him. For a bit. So far, he'd managed to avoid any interactions with his boss, but he didn't anticipate that would last all day. After tomorrow, most of the staff, including Gonzalez, would be out of the office the rest of the week for the Thanksgiving holiday. It was one of the slowest weeks for Nectar, but since Stratford was one of the few skeleton staff members who'd be working all week, it stood to reason he'd have a lot of nonsense dumped on his plate to cover for the others.

"Stratford Dale." He spoke into the receiver with a smile in his voice, glad to see Gonzalez merely grab something from his assistant and step back into his office.

"Stratford Dale, where the fuck have you been?" Abby screeched into the phone.

"Abby, not so loud." Their phones were crap, and the last thing he wanted to do was advertise he was getting a personal call.

"Fine." Abby was quieter, but no less strident. "I waited all damned weekend to get details, and not a fucking word from you. Not even a text."

"You wanted me to text you about my date?"

117

"We already talked about… oh my God. You lying liar-face. I can smell the bonfire that is your pants from here."

It sometimes took until well after lunch before Stratford got the hang of Mondays, and this one was worse because Vinnie had made the weekend exhausting but ever so good. He had no idea what she was talking about.

"Abby, I was just about to go get some lunch."

"I'm waiting downstairs. Unless you're getting some afternoon delight, I'm your lunch date today, buddy."

"Uh, not that I object a lunch date, but what are you doing here?"

"I had an errand to run, and since it brought me right past here, I decided to kill two birds with one stone. In case you missed the subtext… you owe me an explanation, or I'm killing you with a stone."

"An explanation for what?"

"I think I'm going to sleep the rest of the weekend." Abby's tone was mocking. "Sleep. Yeah, right. Who was boning you so much this weekend you couldn't even text me a few details about your reading?"

Stratford tapped the receiver against his temple. How could he have forgotten that? The weekend had been unusually busy, but Vinnie had just consumed his awareness.

"Okay, okay. I'm heading down now."

He slipped past Trey while the guy was on the phone, one bullet dodged, although he suspected Abby might have a hail of them ready and aimed for his head.

AT THE restaurant, after they'd taken off their coats and hung them on nearby hooks, Abby gave him a hug and then stepped back to inspect him. "Looking good, my boy. Relaxed. You need to get laid more often."

Yes, yes he did. No need to dispute that statement, although he didn't feel the need to add that he only wanted to get laid by one particular man.

Once they'd settled into their seats and placed their orders, Abby drummed her fingers on the table. "Talk to me, chicken boy."

Stratford rolled his eyes. Abby only ever called him chicken boy when she was pissed at him.

"Okay, well, the guy I went out with on Friday…."

He then told her everything that had happened since he'd called her to both gush about Vinnie and bitch about his new gig doing Doctor Chicken readings. It took him the entire meal to recount what he considered to be important points. When he finished, he couldn't stop smiling.

"Oh my God, Ford, I love that smile on you."

He didn't have to ask, "What smile?" Thinking about Vinnie broadened his smile and stretched muscles in his face he hadn't used in a long time.

"So, what do you think?"

"Huh. So Bob Marley's a girl?"

Stratford rolled his eyes. "That's all you took away from my story?"

Abby laughed. "No, but it's interesting. I also think you've got some of the craziest luck."

"Don't you mean the worst luck?"

"Well, no. I mean, you've got some bad juju going on to be so spastic in front of a guy you like, but the guy still likes you. Which means your luck isn't all bad."

That made sense, in a weird, Abby-like way. "So, you think he likes me?" Stratford fluttered his lashes and simpered, pretending for all the world that her answer wasn't important.

"Even you can't be that much of a dating idiot. Bring him over this Saturday. No, wait, that's the weekend after Thanksgiving. I'll be too pooped after Black Friday. The Saturday after. It'll be the first barbecue of the Christmas season."

"Didn't I just skip a barbecue last weekend?"

"Yes, but last weekend you were sad and alone and didn't want to bring down our happy couple buzz."

"Sad and alone?" His voice rose an octave, pretending to be shocked by her words. The truth of her words might have stung if it weren't for the fact she would have never said something like that—even joking as she was—if he were truly unhappy now.

119

"Yeah, yeah, bring the new boyfriend by."

"I don't know, Abby. It's a little soon, isn't it?"

"Puhlease! If you ran all potential dates by me before you went out with them, you'd be a lot better off, but this one's already been around for a whole weekend. He just might stick."

Stratford laughed. Abby was deluded if she thought he'd actually do that, but she was probably right, nevertheless.

"I'll ask him, see how he feels about it." Assuming it wasn't just some wild weekend connection, an extended one-night stand. Stratford shook his head. The way Vinnie had treated him all weekend and the sweet things he'd said after the mom debacle gave him confidence that he'd hear from him. Soon. He can't have been the only one caught up in the spell they'd woven together.

"Do that. Maybe I'll make it a dinner party."

Panic fluttered in Stratford's chest. "A dinner party?"

"We have other friends, Stratford. Friends who'd be thrilled to see you with someone who makes you this happy."

Stratford pushed the last bite of tabbouleh around on his plate, nerves constricting his throat just enough that he didn't think he could swallow it. Meeting his friends was a big step, and most of the guys he'd been with hadn't stayed around long enough to bother. As much as he freaked at the thought of officially meeting Vinnie's family—he was going to pretend the underwear incident hadn't happened—he usually wasn't afraid of guys meeting his friends. Vinnie had quickly become important to him, and he wanted Vinnie to like his friends and vice versa.

"Might as well. After all, I've already met his mother."

Abby laughed. "Just make sure you don't leave underwear on my front lawn. Thad might not understand."

Stratford laughed along with her, even as his neck and ears heated. It would be awhile before he'd be able to recall that particular low point in his hapless life without embarrassment.

THE sky was filled with thick, dark clouds that promised flurries at the very least, but Stratford couldn't stop smiling. The morning at work had passed uneventfully, and he'd had a great lunch at a great little falafel place down the street, at Abby's expense. He could talk about Vinnie for hours, and the more he thought about it, the more he liked the idea of Vinnie meeting his friends.

It would be a great night to curl up in front of a fireplace, and for the first time, he could imagine curling up with someone like the scene out of a sappy, romantic movie. If Vinnie stuck around, maybe he'd be able to afford a new apartment with a fireplace. They were out there, especially in some of the older buildings. But that was three years away; even if Vinnie had one at his house, he wouldn't be able to relax enough to make it worthwhile.

A little electric thrill shot through him at the thought of Vinnie still being around in three years. After the weekend they'd had, Stratford could almost believe it possible. The short text, thanking him for a great weekend had "promising" written all over it. He'd replied he'd had a great time, too, but he didn't know if asking Vinnie what his plans were for tonight would be pushing it. Although he'd love to meet up with Vinnie every day, he didn't want to annoy the man, either.

As he entered the building, Barry and Trey were leaving, arm in arm. Drawing strength from their confrontation on the weekend, Stratford squared his shoulders and met their gaze head on. His stomach fluttered, his heartbeat sped up, and he had to battle the very real temptation to fling himself behind the huge planter by the building's entrance. Barry curled his lip in derision and looked away, but Trey sneered at him.

"Where's your rent boy today? Couldn't afford more than a night with him? Did he bust your cherry, or did you chicken out on him too?"

Stratford blinked. He certainly understood Barry's attitude. Even if Barry hadn't been interested in something serious, Stratford had been a little rude about how he'd ended their date. But Trey seemed happy with Barry. It made no sense that anyone could be so sycophantic. What if Stratford's brain and self-esteem completely dribbled out of his ears and he decided he wanted to date Barry again? Would Trey cheer for Barry and him getting together? Ridiculous.

He shook his head. It didn't matter what either of them thought about him.

Trey kissed Barry's cheek, and they bumped into Stratford accidentally on purpose as they passed, their laughter cruel but of no real concern to him. The way his parents had disowned him after coming out made him spend the rest of his life ducking confrontation, afraid of any more rejection. It meant he stayed with guys he shouldn't or stuck it out on dates far too long, as he had with Barry. But even if rejection came, sometimes it didn't matter. Like now. There was no loss for him with Trey and Barry.

He continued to the elevator with no diminishment of his earlier good mood. After all, he'd somehow managed to schedule a few readings over the next month with only minimal begging and wheedling. All he needed to do this afternoon was finish making calls and type up a proposal for his boss. Then just one more day before it would be clear sailing for the rest of the week without any of his headache-inducing coworkers or boss around.

UPSTAIRS, he smiled at Paula and sat down at his desk. His top drawer was ajar, and when he pushed it, it wouldn't close. Yanking open his drawer revealed a package that hadn't been there before he left for lunch. It looked like a box for an action figure. A cutout magazine picture of a pair of shiny, glistening cherries was stuck atop the clear plastic window, obscuring the view. For a moment, a split second, he had a moment of joy. An unexpected gift was an unexpected gift.

Then, he peeled off the magazine page to reveal an enormous bright blue rubbery dildo, whose name was apparently Goliath the Giant. Bastards. The cherries should have been a dead giveaway, but he hadn't even imagined they'd go so far. How the hell was he going to get rid of this?

"Dale? I heard your first reading went well." Gonzalez's voice boomed behind him, and panic sent adrenaline exploding through his veins. He shot out of the chair, fumbling with the package, trying to keep his body between it and his boss while simultaneously shoving it back into his drawer, crinkling and crunching. With a final adrenaline-fueled push, the drawer closed, a ripping sound telling Stratford the dildo was probably now on the loose in his drawer.

He whipped about to face his boss, careful to remain in a protective stance in front of the drawer.

"Uh, Mr. Gonzalez, uh, yes. The reading went fine." Bullshit, but it was easier to say "fine" than tell Gonzalez the truth, especially since the contents of his drawer could probably get him fired.

"The manager reported a significant boost in sales."

Well, yeah, he would, the asshole. Keeping Stratford there an extra hour had probably helped the bottom line tremendously.

"It was certainly busy." Non-committal responses served him well and kept him under the radar.

"Excellent, excellent. Don't forget, I'm expecting your schedule for the rest of your readings on my desk at the end of the day. I want hard dates for the rest of the year, but the ones before launch next year can be tentative." Gonzalez's condescending pat on the shoulder, combined with his magnanimous tone indicated his boss thought he was doing Stratford a favor, but trying to schedule anything this close to Christmas was the true nightmare. Fortunately, he'd already accomplished that Herculean task.

"Of course." His proposal probably wouldn't include anything about his revisions from Saturday's excursion into hell, the marketing brainchild that had almost crippled him.

Gonzalez nodded brusquely before swanning off as though he'd been the one directly responsible for the sales bump.

Letting out the breath he hadn't realized he'd been holding, Stratford let his shoulders relax, and he stood for a moment, allowing his heart rate to return to normal. He slid back into his chair. No question, the poisonous little gift had been from Barry, by way of Trey. No way would Nectar allow non-employees back here where they could—gasp—possibly steal the latest and greatest in the way of greeting-card slogans. Trey had to have been the one to place it in his desk.

He couldn't tell anyone. It was his word against Trey's, and while Gonzalez probably knew he was gay, there was no way Stratford wanted to have it broadcast about the office if he reported this. He didn't even dare try tucking it back into Trey's desk. Knowing him, he'd get caught and not only fired but branded a sexual predator or something.

What the hell was he going to do with it? He grabbed his keys and locked his desk drawer, for the first time in all his years at the company. He would have to continue to do so, if he didn't want any more nasty surprises, but even locked, the drawer seemed to pulse menacingly. It was all he could think about. He'd been planning to schedule his readings for January and February this afternoon, anticipating they'd be much easier than trying to wedge something into the pre-Christmas rush, but now, he wasn't sure he could even concentrate enough to type up the schedule he had been able to arrange.

Fuck.

SOMEHOW Stratford managed to finish his schedule, as well as do some basic editorial work, but the drawer loomed in his thoughts, and he didn't dare leave his desk unattended all afternoon, not even to go to the bathroom. He worked a few minutes later than most of the other office drones, partly because he didn't want anyone to see him open the drawer, and partly because he didn't want to face Trey. This time, it wasn't a fear of confrontation that kept him in his seat, but the very real fear he might actually punch Trey for doing this. Considering how much their bosses sucked, the office was kind of laid back, but an adult sex toy in the desk drawer of the guy who was Doctor Chicken was a professional death knell. No doubt about it.

The office emptied out quickly—no one wanted to stay any longer than they had to—and as soon as his immediate area had cleared out, Stratford grabbed his scarf, yanked open the drawer and wrapped the dildo with its mangled packaging. Shoving it in his messenger bag, he struggled to wedge it in. The bag bulged oddly, but it was secure, and that was all that mattered. He walked swiftly, hoping no one was left to intercept him. He wanted this out of his possession as quickly as possible.

He paused briefly beside Trey's desk, but his luck was universally terrible. If the janitor didn't catch him, the security cameras surely would, even though those same cameras would somehow magically not have caught Trey putting the damned thing in his own desk.

On the way to the elevator, he also considered the trash chute, prying open the elevator doors to toss it down the shaft, and trying to find Barry's desk to leave it there. But he was paranoid—apparently more paranoid than Trey—about anyone seeing him with a fucking dildo. Not that he objected to them in principle, but the office wasn't the place for that. Unless you were fucking the boss. Stratford shuddered at anyone screwing Gonzalez. He'd pitied Mrs. Gonzalez on more than one occasion.

Nowhere was suitable. Every garbage can he saw between the office and home was discarded because of people around to see him dump the dildo. If he was willing to lose his scarf along with the package, that would be one thing, but the days were only going to get colder, and if he was going to take Vinnie out on a date to reciprocate, he was going to need every spare penny.

At his apartment, he considered tossing it in the dumpster behind the building, but at that moment, the doctor's receptionist flounced out of the building, giving him a little wave and giggle. Stratford returned the wave and scuttled upstairs. Maybe later tonight, like midnight, he could sneak out and get rid of it.

Until then, it could stay in the time-honored home of dildos everywhere, so he shoved it in his nightstand drawer. God. The thing was huge. An oversized dick might look great in porn, but Stratford was not interested in hosting a battering ram. Vinnie's above-average cock was going to be more than enough, assuming they got to that point. It had only been a couple of days, but Vinnie hadn't said anything that indicated he felt cheated because they hadn't had anal sex. Not that Stratford had anything against it. He quite liked it, in fact. It was the assumptions and expectations he hated. But Vinnie didn't seem to have any expectations, and even though Stratford would be willing to give anal sex up entirely for the right partner, ironically, that made Stratford want it even more. He was such a head case.

He stared down into the drawer. But he'd never want sex with Goliath the freaky blue Giant. Letting out a snort, he wondered briefly if Nectar had an adult-toy department that had manufactured Goliath the Giant. He and the guy who came up with alliterations for adult toys could get together and commiserate together over a beer.

The chime of a text message on his phone had him slamming the drawer shut, as though the texter could somehow see his new acquisition.

He grabbed the phone. Just the sight of Vinnie's name made him smile.

> *Wanted to see you tonight, but Sienna's got a school recital I forgot about. Sry.*

Stratford's mood deflated.

> *And you said you were busy the rest of the week?*
> *Yeah, Thanksgiving is a zoo around here.*
> *Did you want to come over for Thanksgiving? I know you're working, but you could come over later.*
> *Uh, definitely be too soon for that. No, thank you. I'm expected at Abby's.*
> *Can we talk on the phone this week?*

Stratford couldn't decide if he was upset or pleased by the Thanksgiving invite, but he typed out a quick reply.

> *Sure. Whenever you get the chance, call me.*
> *Promise.*

Vinnie hadn't stayed the night last night, but Stratford hadn't realized how much he wanted to spend the night wrapped in those strong arms. Amazing how quickly he'd come to enjoy sleeping with another person. But the intention apparent in those few words warmed Stratford. Vinnie hadn't forgotten about him and wanted to see him again. That would have to be enough to help him sleep tonight and the next week, along with a date with his hand in a continuous mental loop of Vinnie sucking his cock. Stratford's cock twitched and threatened to plump up right then.

First, though, something that resembled dinner and an evening working on one of his graphic novels or a few sketches.

AFTER Sienna's recital, which had been cuter than cute even if it had been nothing more than barely organized chaos, Vinnie sat on the couch in the living room. For once, he was alone there. Gabriella was getting Sienna ready for bed, then she was going out to a late movie with her boyfriend. His mom was puttering around the kitchen humming, Marissa was going over some contracts in the office, and Evie was studying in her room.

Vinnie smoothed a hand over the couch, remembering the previous day and how quickly a few kisses had Stratford ready to strip down. Having his mother and sister interrupt them had been horrible, especially for those dark few moments when he thought Stratford had given up on him. Vinnie should have thought ahead better. It wasn't fair of him to subject Stratford to that sort of embarrassment, especially since both of them were far too old to get caught making out—or worse—like horny teenagers. Of course, Stratford had him hornier than he ever remembered being as a teenager, but that was beside the point.

He didn't want to keep Stratford away from his family, but he'd rather spend time with Stratford in a place that was as private as Stratford's apartment, specifically one where he could at least cook some pasta and keep Stratford fed. In a few more years, he could get his own place; his family wouldn't be so dependent on him. Maybe he could help Stratford pay for a bigger apartment.

He snorted. There was plenty of time to spring that proposition on Stratford. As much as Vinnie knew he wanted Stratford and thought they'd be great together, he didn't want to scare the man away. After all, they'd only known each other a few days. But for the first time, Vinnie thought there might be something to that love-at-first-sight bullshit. He wasn't in love, but he'd taken one look at Stratford and known, deep in his gut, that Stratford could be the one. Love would come, he was sure of it, but he'd have to consider what shape their relationship would take, given his responsibilities.

Instead of imagining a future with Stratford, or even worse, remembering his sleek body, the taste of his skin, the weight of his cock, because he didn't need to get a woody in the living room where any of his family could surprise him—again—he flipped on the television.

Between managing the shop and growing his company, he'd never had a lot of time for television and had no idea what any of the shows were. He wanted nothing more than to call Stratford, maybe have some phone sex, but for the first time, he felt the confines of his family. No one came into his bedroom uninvited, unless there was fire or blood, but for him to retreat there this early would be cause for curiosity. There was no reason for this tight, uneasy sensation of too many eyes on him, watching.

"Vinnie."

He hadn't even heard his mom enter the room, which only supported his internal argument that getting an erection in the living room was a bad idea.

"Hey, Mama. What's up?"

She rounded the couch with a serious expression on her face. He muted the television to listen to her.

"Did you want to have Stratford over for dinner sometime? Meet the family?"

He bit back the groan. His mom had undoubtedly figured out how serious he was about Stratford for the same reasons Marissa had. But he hadn't even had the exclusivity talk with Stratford yet. He wasn't even sure Stratford had fully forgiven him for yesterday, even though they'd gone to the museum, had dinner, and Vinnie had done his best to apologize with lips and hands in Stratford's shower.

"Mama, I don't know. It's still so soon."

She frowned. "As soon as he's ready." There was no wiggle room. His mom wanted time to grill his boyfriend—or the guy he'd very much like to audition for the role. She'd never had a chance to do it, and suddenly he understood his sisters' irritation when he'd insisted on meeting their guys.

"Yes. Of course."

"Good. He was cute." His mom winked at him, and he squirmed. She laughed and went back to the kitchen.

Thinking of Stratford gave him an idea, and he unmuted the TV and flipped over to Netflix. After a quick search, along with some additional information gathered from the browser on his phone, he assumed Stratford had been talking about the *Doctor Who* episodes that started in 2005. There were a hell of a lot of episodes, but he wanted to find out what Stratford found so fascinating. He started the first one and sat back to watch.

A HAND dropped on Vinnie's shoulder and he jumped.

"Whoa, hey, just saying good night, Vinnie."

Those mannequins coming to life in the first episode had been fucking creepy.

"Good night, Marissa."

She continued to stand behind him, and he paused the show. It hadn't taken him long to get sucked in, and he didn't want to miss anything, although he hadn't seen any bow ties yet.

A big sigh ruffled his hair.

"Come and sit."

Because Marissa was closer to his age than his other sisters—she was only a bit younger than Stratford—he related to her more as a sister than as the pseudo-father-brother thing he had going on with Gabriella and Evie. Their roles were more clearly defined, but she'd still been only twelve when their dad had died. When she'd indicated she wanted to take her MBA and help him with his company, he'd been thrilled. They worked very well together, and after only a few months, he wondered how he'd ever done all the work by himself. Tonight, though, she had something on her mind, and it wasn't difficult to tell she wanted to talk to her big brother, not the CEO.

Marissa sat up close to him and rested her head on his shoulder the way she used to do when they were kids.

"Since when do you watch *Doctor Who*?"

He hadn't expected that question, so he deflected. "Since when do you know about *Doctor Who*?"

She laughed. "Don't you remember Keith?"

Vinnie had to think about that one. Marissa was so levelheaded, he'd never worried about her or the boyfriends she chose. Or at least, no more than any big brother would.

"Keith? He was that geeky kid you dated a few years ago?"

"Yeah, he was a little obsessed by it. That, *Star Wars*, and *Star Trek*. He used to call it the nerd trifecta. I have to admit, I'll watch an episode of the Doctor now and again, because the show is a lot of fun, but I never thought you'd be into it."

Nerd trifecta. Was Stratford into all three? Vinnie did remember liking *Star Wars*, although it had been years since he'd seen it.

"Well...."

"Probably you shouldn't be casting stones at Keith's geekiness, not if you're watching this because of him."

So true. And there was very little point in pretending he didn't know which him Marissa referred to. "But Keith was just weird. Stratford is...." There were so many words to describe Stratford, but Vinnie still had an image to uphold. "Charming."

"Charming. Honestly, Vinnie. The guy was totally hot. I'm pretty sure it's not his charm that's got you hooked."

Since the day he came out, this might be the first time Marissa had ever broached the subject of his sex life, probably because he'd never shown his family he had one until now. Pretty much every discussion about sex in this house had been him warning his sisters about boys and what they wanted and how to protect themselves. Or giving their boyfriends the third degree. The tables had never once been turned on him.

"No, but...." Vinnie stared down at his hands. How did he explain how he felt when he'd never felt like this before?

Marissa grabbed his hand. "Look, Vinnie, I wanted to apologize again."

"For what?"

"For, well, spooking Stratford. I really didn't mean to. And I hope we can meet again under better circumstances, because I can tell how much you care about him."

His whole body tensed. "How can you possibly?"

Marissa laughed. "Look, I think we were all shocked yesterday. But I'm not an idiot. There's no way you've been celibate all these years. Yesterday was the first time… well, as far as I know… that you've brought a guy to the house. And quite frankly, even if you had brought a guy around before for a little something-something, I'm pretty sure you wouldn't have offered to let him do his laundry just so you could spend more time with him. And then there's *Doctor Who*. It has to be serious if it's got you watching television that's not got some sort of educational component to it."

Vinnie grinned, unable to hold it in any longer. "I do… really like this guy."

Shifting on the couch, Marissa gave him a big hug. "I'm so happy for you." Marissa rarely squealed, but her voice had climbed dangerously into squeal range.

"Well, it's early days yet. Probably too soon to know how it will all turn out." Early days or not, he'd still be devastated if Stratford dumped him.

"Pffft. Don't go getting all negative. I know things were weird yesterday, but that guy was 100 percent into you."

"You think?" Vinnie groaned. He'd had too much experience listening to teenage girls fuss about which boys liked them—he knew he sounded exactly like them. He had a few male acquaintances, some friends from his old days working in the shop, but none he'd consider close enough to discuss his relationships with.

"Oh, I think. And I also think he's lucky to have you. He didn't ask you to watch this, did he?" Marissa pointed at the frozen image on the screen.

"No, he didn't."

"Yeah, he's lucky to have you."

Vinnie shook off her praise. It only seemed natural to try to find out what Stratford liked. "So, since you're the closest thing to a *Doctor Who* expert I've got, when does he start wearing bow ties?"

131

Marissa laughed. "This is, what, the third episode you're on? You've got a ways to go."

Vinnie shrugged. The show was good enough he'd probably continue to watch when he had a moment alone with the television.

"Hey, can you do me a favor?"

"After yesterday's, uh, meeting, I think I owe you."

Vinnie smiled and rocked his shoulder into her gently. "You didn't scare the nice man away, so no, you don't owe me. But will you look into Nectar tomorrow? They might be a good investment."

He wanted to know why Stratford wasn't raking it in with his talented work. The man might not have noticed, but the line-up for both his signing and the cash register had been out the door. What he'd seen had only been a small representation of the sheer number of goods available, because he damn well knew Sienna wanted every one as soon as they came out. If it looked like Nectar was doing something shady or if they were about to fold, he wanted to give Stratford some warning.

"Sure thing. Any rush?"

"No, no, take your time." A rush would only cause undue curiosity in his sister. There would be plenty of time to worry about that once Marissa discovered Stratford worked at Nectar.

His sister patted his knee. "Well, I'm going to bed. Please tell Stratford how sorry I am, will you?"

"Sure." He wasn't sure how well Stratford would take it, but maybe after cooking class next week, he'd take Stratford home, do his best to suck the skittish right out of him through his dick, then spring the sister apology on him. The first part of the plan was a given, no matter what. Spending the night apart tonight had been necessary, but that didn't mean he liked it.

Waiting until after cooking class to get Stratford naked would be torture. Torture that was only going to be worse if he kept imagining his hands and mouth all over Stratford. And he was definitely going to warn his mother he was going to be late that night. Staying overnight during the week was another step he shouldn't take without talking it over with Stratford. They'd have to make their schedules work with showering and shaving in Stratford's tiny apartment, and he'd have to explain why he was as dressed up for work as he was for their dates. He didn't wear suits often, but a dress shirt and neatly pressed pants wasn't the customary garb of your average, everyday auto mechanic.

Grimacing, he pressed the play button on the remote. He could probably stay awake for another episode or two, put off worrying how or when he should tell Stratford about his success. He couldn't tell him, not yet. Not until Vinnie was sure Stratford cared for him. Vinnie was good at judging people, and Stratford didn't strike him as a money-grubbing mercenary, but there was only one way to be perfectly certain.

He turned up the volume using the remote, hoping the melodic British accents could drown out the voice of guilt in his head.

Nine

STRATFORD was actually happy to be at work today, if only because he had cooking class after work, and cooking class meant Vinnie. Hopefully without another trip to the urgent care clinic. There weren't any cooking classes during Thanksgiving week, and he'd really missed seeing Vinnie. The phone conversations had been good, almost like minidates. They spoke nearly every day, and Stratford had found out they'd had a lot more in common than he'd thought. By mutual consent, they'd avoided the topic of family or work, but they'd found a ton of other things to talk about and even had a chance for a round of phone sex.

He hadn't seen Vinnie in eight days, and he was practically bouncing, knowing Vinnie would be coming home with him after.

His mood was such he was even able to hold back a glare for Trey as he walked in, despite the cackle of laughter. So infantile, but then Trey was practically in diapers anyway. Stratford wasn't even sure the guy was old enough to drink. Although Stratford might not be thrilled about turning thirty, he was damn happy he didn't act like an adolescent bully.

Paula waved at him, and he waved back before turning his computer on. After a quick inspection of his desk revealed his desk drawer still locked and no other visible land mines like Goliath, he settled down to get to work. Vinnie and his upcoming date kept distracting him. Several times, he realized he'd been staring at his computer for several minutes but not actually seeing anything on the screen. At least he looked like he was being productive, even though all he was doing was thinking about sex and then trying desperately to not think about sex, because getting a hard-on at work was the last thing he wanted.

"Dale. In my office, now." Gonzalez's bellow billowed out of his office and floated across the room.

If Stratford had a tail, he would have tucked it between his legs. That bastard. If he was pissed, he yelled for the offender from his office, even though there was a perfectly functional phone on his desk that Stratford knew the asshole knew how to use. But the subtle humiliation of being called on the carpet wouldn't be complete if the entire office wasn't aware you were going to get your ass handed to you.

Stratford shoved back from his desk. Seeing Vinnie would make this all better, he hoped. Walking toward Gonzalez's office, not one person lifted their head to meet his gaze. None of them wanted to be tarred with his stink. Stratford was rarely called into his boss's office like this. As Doctor Chicken, he had a little more autonomy than most of the other greeting-card grunts. This had to be about that damned dildo. Someone must have seen it. He'd manage to forget about it for the week—out of sight, out of mind—but he really had to trash it. If he got fired over a dildo he got stuck with because of a nasty practical joke, both Trey and Barry were going to be sporting black eyes before he left the building. He'd never hit anyone before, but this would be a damn fine reason to start.

"Yes, sir?" Stratford closed the door behind him and sat. Let the rest of the office speculate about why the shit storm had found him.

Gonzalez threw a pile of paper on his desk near where Stratford sat. He peered at the papers.

"That's the Fish Fables galley."

"Yes, and you told me you proofed it."

"I did."

Gonzalez flipped a couple of pages and stabbed at the text with a stubby nicotine-stained finger.

"What does that say? Read it."

"Polly the bollock… oh." Yeah, that was supposed to have been Polly the pollock.

"I thought it was stupid to put some obscure fish in this story in the first place, regardless of *how nice the double l's look and sound together*." Gonzalez adopted a mocking tone as he mimicked Stratford's original argument for making Polly a pollock fish. "Goddamn it, Dale. You're lucky the mistake was caught before it went to print."

"I'm sorry. I'll try not to let it happen again."

"You better not. There will be no testicles in this Chicken shit."

Stratford was completely and utterly unable to hold in a snicker at his boss's unfortunate choice of words.

But the laugh only made things worse. He bit the inside of his cheek to hold the laughter in, but it was a strain Gonzalez clearly recognized as the man's face darkened. "You think it's funny? One more mistake like that, and I'll fire your ass."

A sudden flash of anger pushed him to his feet. "You can't fire me—I *am* Doctor Chicken."

Stratford's face flamed. Had he seriously just said that? Gonzalez still wasn't laughing now, either. His expression merely became more thunderous.

"No, you're just the pretty face, the front man for the Doctor Chicken enterprise. We can find another Doctor Chicken, one right out of college and pay him less than you. So no more fuckups, or you'll be out on your ear."

Stunned, as though Gonzalez's words had been a blow to the solar plexus, Stratford plopped down in the chair, breathless with fear. He was just a pretty face? Gonzalez was conveniently forgetting that Stratford had developed the idea from nothing, creating books and greeting cards and gifts, and even providing the springboard for an online game. No matter what his contract said, it was all his. His ideas, his creativity, his baby. He might resent the baby now, but he didn't appreciate Gonzalez's threat. The knowledge that Gonzalez had zero appreciation for the contribution Stratford had made to the success of Nectar stung.

The man had to be bluffing. After all, what kind of idiot would agree to work for less than Stratford was making now?

"Get out." His boss flicked the galley at him, uncaring that Stratford had to scramble to catch it. "And no more fuckups."

Dumbfounded, Stratford rose and left the room. Somehow, he managed to close the door behind him with a gentle hand, rather than slamming it with a flourish the way kids always did after getting reprimanded. Again, no one met his gaze with the sole exception of Paula, who gave him a sympathetic little smile.

Gonzalez's door opened behind him with a distinctive whoosh as his mere presence sucked the morale right out of the cubicle farm.

"And change Polly to a Pike. Got that? Revised galley on my desk by the end of day."

End of day? Fuck. Getting to cooking class on time would be a challenge.

No matter the temptation, he'd managed to avoid texting Vinnie five hundred times, but now he had a good excuse, even if the threat to his job made him feel lower than the chicken shit Gonzalez had inadvertently called his work. Or perhaps not so inadvertently. Despite the success of Doctor Chicken, Gonzalez never seemed to have any appreciation for his work.

He picked up his phone to text Vinnie.

> *I might be a little late for class—work issue. Save me a spot?*
> *Of course :)*

Stratford let Vinnie's immediate reply soothe him as he began work on revising the galleys for Fish Fables. Gonzalez expected more than a few red marker adjustments when he referenced a revised galley. Especially since pikes and pollocks were two damned different fish, which meant modifications to the illustrations and some of the associated storyline, never mind having to fight for time at the good printer. At least the illustrations were only cartoonish figures with big googly eyes loosely based on the forms of the original animal. But he'd managed to work in so many lovely double *l*'s in the story. He'd leave those in, because that was the hardest part, and Gonzalez wouldn't care one bit about artistic integrity.

He opened his galley copy and started making notes. How was he going to live like this for three more years? The look on Vinnie's face when he realized Doctor Chicken had barely given Stratford enough to live on had been… shocking. Abby had been telling him to get out of Nectar for a long time, but he'd heard it so many times from her it no longer made much of an impression. Maybe she was right. Maybe he should consider taking her up on her offer of assistance.

It certainly couldn't hurt to send out a few résumés, see what kinds of work were available. Graphic-design jobs had to be available. Hell, if it came down to it, Nectar wasn't even the only greeting-card company that had offices in the area. Nectar had long since passed unbearable, especially with these new public appearances. He had another one on Saturday, and he was dreading it already, even though he had at least made better arrangements than those sadists in the marketing department.

He'd been Doctor Chicken for so long, he just might miss it, but he couldn't do this for three more years.

VINNIE stared up at Stratford's ass as he followed him up the stairs to his apartment. The days since he'd been here had stretched out like an eternity. Somehow, he would contain himself until Stratford had fed Marley, but despite Stratford's stated desire to shower, he didn't think he could bring himself to let the man shower alone.

Cooking class had been fun, despite the mishap with the tikka masala. Stratford had defended his territory against Bethany's attempted intrusions, making Vinnie hard as a rock. For the most part, they'd moved around each other in a graceful dance as though they'd cooked together a million times before, like clothed foreplay. If Vinnie had been able to control himself and not grabbed Stratford's ass with both hands, Stratford probably wouldn't have dumped the tikka masala down his front. The cinnamon bun and latte he'd had ready for Stratford when he'd first arrived in class had put Stratford in a forgiving mood, though.

The guy had a serious sweet tooth, and Vinnie liked being able to feed it.

When they got into Stratford's apartment, Marley tackled their legs, and Stratford let out a few half-hearted curses.

"Does she like to be picked up?"

"Yeah... or well, more to the point that she doesn't object to anything."

Vinnie scooped up the cat, mostly as a way to keep his hands off Stratford while he used kitchen utensils.

By the end of cooking class, he was barely able to taste what was left of the tikka masala because the only thought in his head was about getting Stratford home and naked.

Marley was a nice distraction, though. He liked the solid weight of her along with her boneless compliance and the faint, breathy purrs that escaped with each exhalation. He rubbed his nose against her velvety black one, smiling at the tickling of her whiskers against his face.

Stratford made a strangled noise, and Vinnie looked up to find Stratford staring, eyes wide, mouth slightly hanging open. He wasn't sure he recognized the expression, but he thought it might be longing. Yeah, Stratford wasn't likely to be showering alone.

"What's wrong?"

Stratford shook his head before his expression morphed to his impish, teasing expression Vinnie wanted to see more of.

"Nothing. Just gotta love a guy who loves cats." Stratford set Marley's food on the ground, and to avoid impending disembowelment, Vinnie set Marley on the floor. While he'd fought with Marley, Stratford had slipped out of the kitchen, and Vinnie got one tantalizing glimpse of a wiggling ass before the door closed.

Just as well. He wasn't sure if Marley had managed to get a solid kick in his solar plexus or whether it was Stratford talking about love, but Vinnie had a hard time catching his breath. Wandering into Stratford's bedroom, he picked apart nuances of Stratford's last words. His ears got hot, then flashed cold. Surely Stratford wasn't in love already. That can't have been what it meant. But Vinnie couldn't deny how good it would feel if Stratford was. He'd been barreling along that path at light speed, and he'd always been one to make quick decisions, but this wasn't a business deal or a hiring decision. This was his heart, and snap decision or not, it was a huge fucking gamble.

Still, it's not as though either of them were kids. There wasn't anything wrong with reaching for what they wanted, and Vinnie hoped they wanted the same thing.

He sat at Stratford's desk and perused what appeared to be more sketches for his graphic novels. Gorgeous, like the man himself. In fact, based on the sketches, he'd expected *Doctor Who* to be more superhero oriented. He could probably flip through Stratford's work all day, especially if it kept him from digging for hidden meanings in what may have been no more than a joke.

Discussing it could wait—had to wait—because that hadn't been a declaration by any stretch of the imagination. He was already exclusive in his mind, wanting no one but Stratford from that first day, but he wanted Stratford to feel the same. They'd have to have an exclusivity talk, and soon, before someone realized what a great guy Stratford was. It may be a barbaric, unfamiliar sentiment, but he wanted Stratford to be his alone. He suspected he'd already seen Stratford's clumsy worst and how most of it disappeared when he was happy and calm. Vinnie wanted Stratford happy, although he wasn't sure if it was possible to keep him calm at the same time he was so turned on he was ready to crawl out of his skin. Calm might not be as high on the agenda.

Antsy over his decision, still horny as hell, and feeling a bit like he was snooping, Vinnie stood and paced. How long was Stratford going to be in the shower? Vinnie liked tikka masala just fine. Licking it off Stratford's chest would be no hardship at all.

Pacing in Stratford's tiny bedroom did nothing to bleed off his restlessness. He sank down on edge of the bed. Television might be enough of a distraction, and he pulled open the drawer on the bedside table. The remotes he recalled seeing the other night were obscured under what appeared to be—despite the battered box—a brand-new dildo. A brand-new, bright blue, dildo called Goliath. And it certainly was. Vinnie was fairly well-endowed, but Goliath put him to shame. Was this what Stratford wanted? Why had Stratford bought the thing now?

Vinnie couldn't stop staring. Against his will, he reached in and pulled out the box, turning it over in his hands, barely able to read how good Goliath was supposed to make someone feel. Vinnie loved everything, although oral—giving and receiving—edged out a lot of other ways to orgasm. In many ways, he found it more intimate, more intense than anything else, and with a partner like Stratford, coming had just about blown the top of his head off. Every damned time, even their first time in the car.

His arousal wilted like week-old lettuce as the words formed in his brain. Had Stratford been so badly disappointed by their sex he'd gone and bought this out of desperation?

"Oh, shit." Stratford's voice was loud in the silent room, and Vinnie almost jumped of the bed. He had been so stunned by Goliath that he hadn't even heard the shower turn off.

Stratford grabbed at the box, almost losing the towel wrapped around his waist, but Vinnie's hands were clenched and locked around it.

"Is this…." Vinnie's voice cracked, and he cleared his throat before trying to speak again. "Is this what you want? Something you… missed out on since we started seeing each other?"

God. He wanted Stratford to be happy, but it had never occurred to him that what had seemed organic and natural to him might not have been Stratford's thing.

Stratford clenched his fists in the white terrycloth, tying it more firmly around his waist. Scarlet streaked up his chest and into a face framed by unruly wet locks. Vinnie's cock twitched. Even as shell-shocked as he was, he'd probably always be entranced by Stratford blushing, especially now that he realized the fierce ones started below the collar.

Those big brown eyes danced, avoiding Vinnie's gaze yet again… but this time only for a few interminable seconds. Still flushed, Stratford drew in a deep breath and stepped close to Vinnie, gaze firmly fixed on his eyes. Without looking, Stratford grabbed the box and tore it from Vinnie's grasp, tossing it over his shoulder.

"Vinnie, I had the best time last weekend. And we had some great conversations this past week. I feel like we know each other so much better now. I've missed out on nothing. Nothing. That… thing." Stratford rolled his eyes. "Okay, it's not like I object to dildos or anything, but that one was a gift from Barry."

The sneer in Stratford's voice as he said Barry's name didn't prevent Vinnie's mood from plunging even further. Because a dildo was a damned intimate gift to give to just anyone. Was Stratford still seeing Barry? Had he lied about having just one terrible date to put Vinnie off the scent? This couldn't be a ploy between the two of them to get Vinnie's money; he was well-off, but not well-off enough to induce that kind of conspiracy. He didn't think.

"Okay, whoa, I don't know what the hell you're thinking right now, but I'm the one who's got the bundle of neuroses and oh-so-unattractive self-esteem issues. But I can blame my parents for them. If both of us end up the same way… we're going to be a hot mess."

Somehow, Vinnie hadn't quite expected this take-charge side of Stratford, but he liked it. As long as he wasn't also taking charge with Barry.

"You're not seeing him, are you?" Vinnie almost rolled his eyes too. He was rarely this unsure about anything, but this thing between them was so hot and frantic and overwhelming he was having trouble reacting with anything but his emotions.

Stratford let out a short laugh, an abbreviated version of the sweet laugh that even now made Vinnie want to grab him and kiss him. With a little smile on his face, Stratford stepped between Vinnie's knees and stroked his face with one hand in a move that was already familiar and comforting. Fresh out of the shower, Stratford didn't smell like anything except clean and male, and Vinnie didn't know what he'd do if he had to give Stratford up. After so few days, it shouldn't matter, but letting go would rip his insides to shreds.

"No, I'm not seeing Barry. There's no way he compares to you. That dildo was…." Stratford shook his head in exasperation. "Him and Trey have been teasing me a bit at work, saying I left Barry at that club because I'm a virgin and was scared. And before you ask, no, I'm not a virgin."

Anger flared to sluggish life underneath Vinnie's upset. "So why the dildo?"

"I don't know. They're twentysomethings with a twelve-year-old's sense of humor. It came with a big cutout picture of a pair of cherries. Presumably they were telling me I could pop mine with old Goliath. The thing that pissed me off is that they left the thing at work, in my drawer. My boss almost saw it, and if he had, I'd have been fired for sure."

"Assholes. Why didn't you report it?"

Stratford made a dismissive noise. "I'm pretty sure Gonzalez wouldn't give a hot damn."

The anger pulsed hotter. "That might even be classified as sexual harassment. You need to stand up for yourself."

Vinnie had gone a little too far with that last statement, judging from the slight glare he got from Stratford.

"My boss hates me and the work I do. I'm sure I'd get blamed for it. He threatened to fire me today, for a simple mistake. I rarely make mistakes, but this one was… a doozy."

Fired? Vinnie had to find out more about this company, find a way to protect Stratford from this idiot boss.

"I'll tell you about it later, it was actually kinda funny." Stratford had moved his hand to Vinnie's neck, playing with the top button of his shirt.

The subtle movement under Stratford's towel effectively erased both Vinnie's anger and despondency, but the concern he wasn't giving Stratford what he wanted and needed remained.

"And have you been missing out on, uh, dildos?" Not the smoothest way to ask, but he couldn't quite figure out how to ask without making it sound either that he was expecting anal sex or that he didn't like anal sex.

He did like how Stratford became very sure of himself in the face of Vinnie's uncertainty.

"Here's the thing, Vinnie." Stratford knelt in front of him and began unbuttoning his shirt. "I like the real thing. I've never been a fan of the mock cock."

Vinnie's lips twitched as he got a sudden picture of the sweet Doctor Chicken reciting a vastly different type of story, just for him.

The rhyming and alliteration Stratford seemed fond of had to be an occupational hazard.

Stratford wiggled his eyebrows and pushed Vinnie's shirt off his shoulders before starting on his pants as Vinnie's renewed erection fought against the fabric's confines.

"But I love what we've done. If we have anal sex, great. I like it. But if we never do anything besides what we've already done, I won't feel like something's missing. An orgasm is an orgasm, and the ones you give are...." Stratford paused a moment to shiver, his lids lowering in sweet remembrance. "They're spectacular."

Stratford's bare hand on Vinnie's erection dispersed the last of his uneasiness, leaving intense lust in its wake.

He growled and pulled Stratford up, rolling them so they were both on the bed. He was too eager to get to Stratford, and he stripped the towel away to remind him exactly what kind of orgasms he could wring with mouth and tongue.

STRATFORD relaxed on the bed, covered in sweat, pulse pounding. Vinnie kept blowing his damn mind with his blowjobs.

"Fucking fantastic," he managed to wheeze out. Vinnie had collapsed face first beside him after messing up his sheets. Not that Stratford objected. He loved how out of control Vinnie got just from sucking him off, but he was going to have to find a way to work a few more sheet sets into his budget even if Vinnie only came over every other day.

The traces of uncertainty that had been there before they had sex were gone, replaced by a well-earned, smug male satisfaction.

"Yes, you were." Heedless of their sweat-slicked bodies and wet spot, Vinnie hauled him close before kissing his ear. "I don't want to leave yet, but if I stay here like this, I'm going to fall asleep."

"Would that be so bad?" Waking up next to Vinnie was an activity Stratford would like to repeat many, many times.

"Not at all, but are we ready for mid-week sleepovers? They require toothbrushes and changes of clothes and sharing the bathroom in a compressed time frame."

"Yeah, I know." A whisper of something—fear or anticipation—slid through him, sending a shiver down his spine. Was he ready for that? "I wouldn't mind trying."

"Me neither. Maybe soon."

Stratford relaxed into Vinnie's side, rubbing his fingers lightly on Vinnie's lightly furred stomach. Maybe this would be a good time to broach Abby's demand.

"What are you doing Saturday?"

"You have another Doctor Chicken appearance?"

Oh, yeah, that. "Yes." He sounded about as enthused as he felt.

"Well, then, I'm going to be there." Vinnie hugged him tighter.

"You bringing Sienna again?"

"Nope. I'm going there to support you, and if you overdo it again, I'm going to take care of you. If you don't, we can go out for dinner again or something. Either way, we're going to have a repeat of this." Vinnie waved a hand at the drying wet spot on the sheets.

The dread he'd had about his next reading eased some, knowing Vinnie would be there to support him, although he was hoping he'd made enough alterations to the event to avoid the necessity of Vinnie babying him like a helpless infant.

There was only so much of that he could handle without completely losing all self-respect, even if the massage had been incredible. Since Vinnie had already seen him at his worst, today's debacle just another layer of icing on the cake, it was a wonder he had even a shred of self-respect left to worry about, but he didn't want to be some helpless, geeky idiot Vinnie pitied.

"Well, I hope I won't end up like I did last time. My best friend Abby and her boyfriend Thad are having a dinner party. Nothing formal or anything—Thad's obsessed with barbecuing—but we're both invited."

"I'd love to go." Vinnie's prompt response and lazy smile were just more reasons for Stratford to fall for the guy. This was all happening crazy fast, but he didn't want to put the brakes on, he wanted to speed ahead.

"Okay, good."

They lay there, but Vinnie had an expectant air about him, as though there was something he wanted to say. For once, though, Stratford didn't worry about the rejection; he had no urge to run anywhere. He was slowly beginning to trust Vinnie wasn't going to reject him, and he was able to relax a bit, find the humor in his foibles.

But he could only wait so long, wondering what Vinnie had to say. "Out with it."

"Out with what?"

"You've got something on your mind. Spit it out so we can relax. Or...." Stratford brushed a finger over Vinnie's quiescent cock.

"Hmm. I might be persuaded to engage in some 'or' before I have to go." Vinnie grinned, but the slight tension hadn't disappeared.

Stratford rolled onto his side, giving him a better angle to stare penetratingly at Vinnie, use the Force to get him to speak.

Finally he did. "I know you said you didn't want to talk about this, but I don't understand your job. I don't understand how come Doctor Chicken hasn't made you, personally, more financially sound. It sounds awful, doesn't it? Because I don't care whether you've got money or not, but it bothers me that you're not getting what you deserve. You're a smart, talented man who shouldn't have to scrape by the way you do."

Huffing in irritation, Stratford flopped onto his back again. Vinnie was determined to learn every humiliating fact about him. Given what Vinnie had seen and heard since they met, this one bit shouldn't matter. And if it was all out there, and Vinnie didn't leave, maybe Stratford could trust this mad rush of feeling, give into it and enjoy the dizzying rush of falling for a truly good man.

"Doctor Chicken was probably the most epically bad decision in my history of bad decisions."

There was a tiny snort from Vinnie's direction, but Doctor Chicken was one of the few decisions Stratford had made that he still wasn't able to laugh about. Not while it was both his livelihood and a stranglehold on his creativity.

Vinnie must have realized that Stratford wasn't kidding, and waited for him to speak.

"The thing you don't understand is that Nectar isn't a publishing company in the traditional sense. It's a greeting-card company. I told you I started working there out of college, right?"

Stratford didn't bother to see if Vinnie nodded, he just continued talking.

"I've always wanted to create graphic novels—write them, draw for them, even do the layout. There was no way Nectar was going to help with that, but they might be useful in another way. I came up with an idea for Doctor Chicken and pitched the idea. I thought getting experience in a very similar process from start to finish would give me the experience to do what I really want to do."

Now, he could only thank whatever benevolent spirit had been looking out for him that Nectar hadn't been the right fit for his superheroes. It would have killed him to lose rights to them.

"It was only supposed to be temporary. A learning experience." Stratford ground his teeth together. Years he'd devoted to the damned company. "So it didn't matter to me that the contracts they wrote up didn't offer things like royalties. Didn't give me rights over the Doctor Chicken name or characters."

The entire Doctor Chicken enterprise had been his fucking idea, and all he got was a salary that barely kept him fed and a job that sucked the life out of him.

Vinnie was a smart guy, and it didn't take him long to realize what Stratford had lost out on.

"You don't get royalties. And I guess the contracts say Nectar hold the rights to the name and characters. So, even though it was your idea, you're essentially the Doctor Chicken ghostwriter. You can't even take Doctor Chicken to a different company."

"Yes, that's about it." Not that he wanted to be saddled with the Doctor Chicken moniker forever. That would be a hundred kinds of hell.

"What about the greeting cards? Toys? Hell, the online game they've been advertising for months."

"Ugh. I don't want to even think about it. I write the greeting cards. I provided specs and sketches for the toys. I came up with the game idea and provided most of the character images for it."

Vinnie gasped, and Stratford resolutely didn't look at him. He spent a good deal of time pretending the line wasn't nearly as successful as it was, because if he thought about it too long, it made him sick.

"Why haven't you fought this? I'm sure a decent lawyer could get those contracts overturned. Or at least get you a percentage of the profits."

"Fight it? Last I looked, lawyers cost money. And besides, at this point, I think I hate Doctor Chicken. Coming up with those stories and images on demand is creatively draining, especially when the boss thinks it's no different than creating mass-market picture frames, one after the other, on a conveyor belt. Sometimes, that's what it seems like I'm doing. Cookie-cutter crap on demand."

"Stratford, I had no idea. I'm appalled that they took advantage of you that way—and still do. I understand why you made the decision originally. You're selling yourself short, though. I've read almost all of those Doctor Chicken books. Sienna is a total fan, there's no joke about that. What you've done, what you've continued to do is write fun, clever stories where kids learn something. I'm in awe of your talent, I truly am."

Maybe Doctor Chicken wasn't so terrible after all. Not when it garnered such sincere and heartfelt praise from a guy like Vinnie. Stratford smiled, just a bit. And he appreciated Vinnie not telling him he was an idiot. He knew that already.

"If you're not going to fight, maybe you should just get another job."

As difficult as it would be to leave Doctor Chicken behind, Stratford had already come to that conclusion. A few years too late, but slow was better than never.

"Abby has been telling me that for a long time." But Stratford didn't want to tell Vinnie or Abby he'd spent most of the weekend revamping his résumé and sending it out to a ton of places. Not until he saw if anyone was interested in him.

"She sounds like a smart woman. I can't wait to meet her."

Stratford dredged up a tiny smile, but discussing his job gave him the same slight stomach upset he experienced almost every day, nine to five. Or six. Or seven, as were the vagaries of Gonzalez's demands.

"Hey, I'm sorry. That was a shitty discussion, and we'd been having a great night." Vinnie kissed his shoulder, but Stratford wasn't even sure he was up for sex. Not right now.

"I don't talk about it much. Abby knows, which is part of the reason she keeps bugging me about it." And one of the reasons he kept ignoring her. Sticking his head in the sand was just easier. "Don't you have to get going?"

Stratford could have kicked himself for the petulance of his tone.

"Oh, no. Not getting rid of me when you're like this. I want to leave you with good memories. Why don't you put on some *Doctor Who*? We can watch an episode, then maybe I'll see if I can put you in an even better frame of mind."

With Vinnie's dark coloring, he looked quite sinister and devious, but utterly sexy.

"We can watch something besides *Doctor Who*."

"Nah, I started watching it last week, in between family obligations. I'm halfway through the first season. I'm really enjoying it."

Stratford wasn't sure he could breathe. Had Vinnie started watching it because of him? That was sweet on a level he'd never experienced in any guy he'd ever met. A swell of happiness filled him, coaxing his lips into a wide grin.

Vinnie smiled back, gave him a kiss, and settled back, waiting for Stratford to queue up a DVD.

Ten

THEY paused in front of Abby's front door, and Stratford squeezed Vinnie's hand to reassure him, although it wasn't Vinnie who needed the reassurance.

Vinnie brushed a kiss over his temple, and Stratford manned up and rang the bell. Abby would have to love Vinnie because Stratford was falling fast. This wasn't the infatuation he'd experienced with his other boyfriends—quick to ignite and even faster to fizzle out. This was deeper—and scarier—but for the first time he *believed* he might have found something lasting, not merely had the hope of such. It was early days, but Vinnie was different from any other guy he'd dated.

Although they hadn't graduated to midweek sleepovers yet, he and Vinnie had seen each other every night since Tuesday's cooking class and had spent the afternoon at a nearby mall, in another Nectar store for a Doctor Chicken event. Coming to Abby's house together only cemented how much like a couple they felt. Did Vinnie feel the same way?

Thad opened the door with a smile. "It's about time you got here. Abby's been predicting you'd blow us off."

Stratford raised his eyebrows. "Blow you off? No thanks. I've hit my quota for the day."

He grinned when Thad rolled his eyes and punched him on the shoulder. "Whatever." Thad turned to Vinnie. "Hi, I'm Thad."

"Vincent. Vinnie, actually."

"C'mon in. Dinner's almost ready, and the others are already here."

Pasting on a confident smile, Stratford led Vinnie inside. Abby had promised outdoor barbecue and other couples to take the heat off introducing Vinnie to his friends for the first time, which was the only reason he felt comfortable subjecting Vinnie to Abby this early in the game. They followed Thad into the kitchen.

"I brought some cannoli." Vinnie handed Thad a bakery box, still tied.

Thad inspected the box and then looked at Stratford. "How'd he make sure you didn't get into this yet?"

"What? I have some self-control." Stratford was trying to fight the blush, but he knew he'd failed when Vinnie laughed. Vinnie had picked up on his sweet tooth pretty damn quickly, but every time Vinnie surprised him with a scone or a cinnamon bun or even a latte, it gave Stratford the warm fuzzies inside.

"I brought him a couple in a separate bag."

"Well, that explains the 'I just had a snootful of coke' look he's sporting."

Blood rushed to Stratford's face so fast he got a mini–head rush, and he scrambled to wipe at his upper lip.

Vinnie stepped in front of him and cupped his face in his hands. "He's just teasing you. Remember this?"

The kiss Vinnie planted on him was deep and sweet and sexy enough that Stratford had to suppress the urge to throw himself into Vinnie's arms and beg to find a bed. And it was just as powerful as the kiss they'd shared in the car.

"No sugar was going to survive that, right?" Vinnie gave him an exaggerated leer before he licked the skin between Stratford's mouth and nose, making him giggle.

Then he punched Thad's shoulder before he bent to rearranging stuff in the fridge, laughing all the while.

"Oh, man, the look on your face." Thad proffered them both beer bottles, still smirking. Stratford grabbed one with a huff. It would take more than a beer to get him to forgive Thad.

151

"C'mon, Vinnie. Let me introduce you around." It had been so long since he'd wanted to introduce a man to his friends.

Vinnie grabbed the beer Thad was holding, gave him a nod, and let Stratford lead him into the living room.

Abby looked up and squealed. How much had she had to drink? Not that she wasn't always excited to see him, but the squealing was a little excessive.

Bounding off the couch, she darted toward them. "Vince!"

Vinnie set his beer down on a nearby table, then suddenly, Abby was in Vinnie's arms, and they were hugging and smiling. Stratford took a step back, jealousy and confusion and irritation swirling into a sickening mix that snuffed out his earlier happiness. Everyone in the living room came to a dead, silent stop as they watched Abby positively *maul* his soon-to-be boyfriend, if he had anything to say about it.

He also wasn't sure he liked Abby calling Vinnie *Vince*. A glance at the kitchen doorway revealed Thad looking... unimpressed. He wasn't exactly upset; more like he didn't know what to think about this turn of events. Catching Stratford's eye, he lifted an eyebrow in question. Stratford shrugged. As much as he wanted to scream and tear Vinnie away from Abby, a queeny fit of jealousy wasn't going to make this situation better. Hell, they'd only been dating for almost three weeks. Letting out his inner jealous bitch was only going to have Vinnie running the other way.

Abby slid out of Vinnie's embrace but still stood far too close to him, one hand resting lightly on his arm, while she stared up into his face. "Vince, you look great."

"Thanks, Abby, you do too. When Stratford told me about his friend Abby, it never even occurred to me that it might be you."

"Holy shitballs! *You're* Ford's Vinnie? I don't fucking believe it." Abby tossed a shocked look at Stratford before turning her attention back to Vinnie. Apparently she'd misinterpreted Stratford's get-your-hand-off-my-man glare because she put *both* hands on his arms and smiled up at him.

"Guilty as charged, I'm afraid."

"Shut up. Really?" Abby pushed at Vinnie, but didn't succeed in putting nearly enough space between them. Stratford had no idea what to do, but he badly wanted to do something.

Vinnie shrugged. "How are you doing, Abs? I met Thad a few minutes ago. Seems like you got yourself a great guy there."

Abs? No, no, that would never do.

"Uh-huh. Yes, I do." Was Stratford imagining things? It seemed her voice didn't have the conviction in it she normally had when telling everyone about Thad, which was just about when the man in question began to frown.

Vinnie glanced at him, a wide smile curling those sexy lips. Stratford tried to respond, but his shocked muscles had a hard time simulating a pleased expression.

"We'll have to catch up." Vinnie gave Abby another hug.

Stratford put his beer on the same table where Vinnie left his so he wasn't tempted to throw it across the room.

"Yes. You still got the shop?"

"Sure. It's doing well, we've even expanded over the years."

"Good for you."

"Um, excuse me." Stratford couldn't bear to watch the tender reunion for another millisecond. "Just how do you know each other?"

If Stratford had ever seen a Cheshire-cat grin on a person, Abby had one now. "Ford, honey, meet Vince, my high-school boyfriend."

Thad's eyebrows drew together even as Stratford thought his heart might stop beating. "Your high-school boyfriend?" His voice squeaked as he spoke the last word. Unbelievable. He stared at Vinnie, whose happy expression dulled a bit as he realized how unhappy Stratford was and just how awkward this was playing out in front of his friends.

"Uh, yeah. We were steadies for… about three years."

"I thought I was going to marry the big lug." Abby grinned again, but this time, Stratford imagined he could see the fangs of a predator gleaming in her mouth. Like a big cat, she was toying with his emotional state before she pounced and ripped his heart out.

"Marry?" Thad said the word at the same time as Stratford, thankfully obscuring his continued inability to speak without squeaking.

Abby shrugged. "Sure. Foolish teenage dreams. I had no clue he was gay, though. We, uh…."

Uh. Stratford knew what *uh* meant in Abby-speak. They'd knocked boots. In fact, he remembered Abby telling him once her high-school boyfriend had been her first, and his face flamed as an unwelcome image arose of Vinnie and Abby naked and twisted together. Judging from Vinnie's slightly bashful look and Thad's darkened countenance, Stratford wasn't the only one who was familiar with that particular lexicon of Abby's.

A light cough, loud in the sudden silence of their drama reminded him this farce was playing out in front of an audience. And Stratford had spent a lot of time and effort to avoid appearing vulnerable—to anyone. He wasn't ready to do that in front of anyone, even his friends.

"Stratford, I insist you date my ex-boyfriend. He's a great guy." If anything, her Cheshire-cat grin got more Cheshirey. Bitch. The rest of the room erupted in snickers, and if Stratford had any blood anywhere besides his face, he couldn't tell from the heat in his cheeks. It wasn't even that he couldn't see the humor in the situation, because he could. He just wished it was happening to someone else.

"Well, it's a little incestuous, but I'll take you up on that. But you didn't train him very well. I've had to break a few bad habits that I assume are your fault." Stratford mimed a blowjob, and everyone laughed, except for an affronted "Hey," from Vinnie.

Appalled, he turned his gaze to Vinnie. In front of a roomful of people, he'd essentially announced that the man he wanted as his boyfriend gave inferior blowjobs. Which was so far from the truth Stratford could almost pop just from the memory of Vinnie on his knees.

"Um." Stratford was tempted to scuff his feet like an abashed schoolboy, but he wasn't a boy, he was a grown man who had completely and totally fucked up. With witnesses.

"Way to go." Abby laughed. "I'm going to go help Thad finish up dinner while you dig yourself out of *that* one." She herded her boyfriend into the kitchen.

Fuck, fuck, fuck. He'd never been very good at apologies, but Vinnie deserved one, even after getting a little too up close and personal with his best friend.

"Introduce me to your friends." Vinnie's voice was calm and even. Stratford searched his eyes for any trace of anger or resentment. He saw nothing at all. Would he end up introducing Vinnie to his friends, only to have this be the last night they spent together?

Pressing his lips together, Stratford nodded and guided him around the room. Vinnie dealt good-naturedly with the few jibes that came his way, but Stratford didn't think that in any way exonerated what he'd done.

Three other couples there, two gay and one straight. In the blink of an eye the introductions were done.

Stratford pulled Vinnie aside. "Want to go out on the porch?" Might as well make it easy for Vinnie to leave without any fanfare. Stratford could catch a cab home after Vinnie left, and he could text Abby about his early departure. Because he sure as fuck wasn't going back inside seconds after getting dumped.

Vinnie nodded.

They hadn't even gotten around to removing their jackets, so that made it all the more convenient. Stratford wrapped his arms around himself. Had the temperature dropped several degrees in the fifteen minutes since they'd arrived, or was that purely a physiological reaction to the dread of losing Vinnie?

"I'm so sor—"

Stratford's heartfelt apology was silenced by Vinnie's invading tongue as his lips were taken in a bruising, hungry kiss that stole Stratford's breath along with the bones in his legs. He wasn't about to look this gift horse in the mouth, although he might kiss it for hours if he could. Stratford pressed himself against Vinnie's solid body, moaning at the sensation of Vinnie's erection rubbing against his own. Jerking his hips, he tried to get as close as he could, but Vinnie pushed him back, the cold night air chilling him.

"What? I mean, why?" Stratford fingered his puffy lips in wonder. "Aren't you mad?"

Vinnie gave him a little indulgent smile, as if he thought Stratford was being cute. He was six feet tall and almost thirty, for God's sake. He wasn't cute, and yet there wasn't any doubt that Vinnie thought he was.

"Did that kiss seem like I was mad?" Vinnie adjusted his dick behind a fly that strained to contain it. "Or does this seem like I'm mad?"

"Then why did we stop?"

Vinnie tilted his head toward the door. "Did you want to go back in there and eat after coming in your pants? I know I don't."

"No. But, I mean… you want to stay? After what I said?"

"C'mere." Vinnie grabbed his hand and sat him down on the two-seater porch rocker that, until now, Stratford had thought the most useless piece of furniture in the world.

Vinnie wrapped an arm around his shoulders, pulling him close, and for a few minutes they watched the twinkling Christmas lights on the house across the street.

"I wasn't trying to make you jealous in there."

Stratford stiffened, wanting to deny he'd been jealous but unwilling to outright lie. He cleared his throat; he should say something, but Vinnie continued, not giving him a chance.

"I didn't even realize you were jealous at first. When I realized you were…. My God, Stratford, I could have bent you over the couch and done you right there. So fucking hot."

Not the most romantic scenario, perhaps, but the heat and eroticism of the statement didn't do a damn thing to deflate his erection.

"Uh, good?"

Vinnie squeezed him a little tighter. "And I know you were just teasing Abby when you maligned my blowjob skills. If you hadn't looked so horrified, I was going to laugh. I haven't spoken to Abby since high school, but I doubt she's changed much since then. If you don't stand up for yourself, she'll walk all over you."

"Yeah, about high school…."

"Yes, we dated. Yes, we had sex. She was my first and only experiment in heterosexuality. My father wouldn't have understood. The guys at the shop wouldn't have understood. The wrestling team wouldn't have understood. Maybe I'm wrong about that, but at the time, I wasn't willing to risk it."

"Sure, I get that." And he did. He'd pretended too, until he went to college, although he hadn't actually done the deed with a girl.

"Right, well, then, I told you my dad died, right? I had to spend every spare minute at the shop trying to support the family. My sisters were twelve, five, and two. There was no way my mom could go back to work. Even though I knew, deep down, that I wasn't into women, I didn't have time for a relationship of any kind. So I broke up with Abby and we went our separate ways. It would have happened eventually, regardless. But I like her. You couldn't have a better friend, and I'm glad you met her."

"Me too. I was in a pretty bad place when I met her. Right before I moved here to go to college, I told my parents I was gay. I was nineteen and so fucking naive. Fortunately, I'd already packed for the dorm and had a bus ticket, because my parents gave me an hour to get out. They were deeply religious, but I was their only child and a bit of a miracle because they'd thought they couldn't have kids. I was kind of spoiled, and it never occurred to me that it would all go away if I told them the truth."

Hugging him close, Vinnie warmed him. Stratford clung to Vinnie's strength. He rarely told anyone about how he met Abby, but he wanted Vinnie to know, and not just because Vinnie knew Abby from before.

"Anyway, I spent the night in the bus station and came here, only to find that I was still painfully and stupidly naive. My parents had pulled their funding. I had a week to come up with tuition and residence fees. I didn't have enough time to apply for loans, I was going to have to forfeit my spot in college, and I didn't have anyplace to live. I had a duffle bag full of clothes and about forty dollars in my wallet. I don't think I've ever been so low in my life. Abby had started her graduate work that semester and was working in the loan office at the school part-time as an administrative assistant. She saw how upset I was when I was leaving the office and managed to get the whole story out of me, in between blubbering."

Stratford sniffed, hoping there wasn't going to be a repeat of those tears. It had been a long time ago, and even though he'd developed a knee-jerk assumption that he was going to be rejected in every situation, he'd more or less made his peace with his parents' abandonment.

"She let me crash at her place until I was able to get myself together. It took me a year and a half before I was able to get a decent job, get the appropriate loans, get myself re-enrolled, and find an apartment. Abby didn't have a lot of money back then either, but she saved my life. It took me longer than normal to get my degree because the loans weren't quite enough to support me, so I had to cut back on classes and work more, but I did it all on my own. After I graduated, I got a job at Nectar and got an apartment with no roommates. Then my school loan repayment kicked in, and I moved to this apartment."

"I'm really proud of you. That took a lot to keep going on your own, and I owe Abby." Vinnie's fingers tangled in his hair and helped soothe away some of his tension.

"It's nothing like you, though. You took care of your whole family. You still do."

"Sure, but I already had the shop to provide for us. It meant giving up college, but my dad supported us with the shop, stood to reason I could too. After my dad died, my mom asked me if I was gay. She's a devout Catholic, but she never once thought about disowning me. So I was already light-years ahead of you, in terms of support. But I don't understand. You're what, twenty-nine? I understand the Doctor Chicken thing hasn't gotten you the money I feel it should."

Stratford tensed again. Vinnie had been so angry when he'd confessed about how his contracts worked for the Doctor Chicken products. Furious, in fact. But he waited, hoping if he didn't say anything, Vinnie wouldn't continue. He shivered a bit, feeling the chill of the air more now that he wanted to run and hide, as he normally did.

"Surely you should be in a better place than this. I mean, you did say that you at least get regular raises, right?"

158

This time Stratford did let a tear trickle out but scrubbed it away, hopefully before Vinnie saw.

"A couple of years ago, I'd saved up enough to pay off my loans in full. I hadn't wanted to increase the payments in case something happened and I couldn't afford the higher rate, but living frugally allowed me to scrape together the thousands of dollars I needed. Then I stupidly allowed my boyfriend at the time access to one of my accounts. He said he needed help to cover some unexpected expenses. But he managed to use the access I'd given him and opened up the rest of my accounts. I hadn't realized that the unexpected expenses he'd referred to were debts owed to his drug dealer. After he paid that off, he took the rest and blew it on rent boys and cocaine. I hadn't known a damn thing about it until the cops came and told me he'd overdosed."

He'd grieved for Ian then. Now he wondered how he could be so stupid. Now he was constantly on alert for signs of drug use or other addictions, and he'd nipped more than one promising date in the bud for precisely those reasons. Stratford might be freaked as hell about the presence of Vinnie's family, but his devotion to them and his responsibilities only made him more appealing, even though he was wary of Vinnie's attempts to try to solve his problems for him.

"Jesus, Stratford." Vinnie pulled him atop his lap and wrapped strong arms around him. "Let me guess. Abby helped you through that too."

"Yes. She offered to give me money to cover my rent and expenses for the month, but I couldn't just take her money. I took a second job for a few months, got an extension on my school loans, and paid her back as soon as I could. So that's why I'm still in that apartment at almost thirty. Three more years on the loans and I'm done."

"This is exactly why you should ask for a bigger piece of the Doctor Chicken revenue. You've certainly earned it."

"Vinnie, please, I don't really want to talk about this now." If he found another job, he'd never have to think about Doctor Chicken again.

The air shifted as Vinnie released a sigh. Silence wove tendrils around them, but Vinnie's arms hadn't loosened at all, and Stratford was able to relax.

Vinnie kissed him, his lips surprisingly warm and soft against Stratford's wind-chilled cheek. "So, *Ford*?"

"So, *Vince*?" Stratford almost laughed, he was so relieved Vinnie had decided to tease him instead of pushing about Doctor Chicken again.

"Okay, okay. During high school, I thought Vince made me sound more grown up. Now, I usually use Vincent for business or when I'm meeting people for the first time. Vinnie is for friends and family."

The explanation went a long way to soothe the anxiety swirling in Stratford's belly. With a guy like Vinnie, it wasn't unprecedented to worry about him deciding to fall back into heterosexuality. "You introduced yourself to me as Vinnie."

Stratford got a little nibble on his neck, making him shiver, before Vinnie answered. "The second I saw you, I knew I wanted to be more than acquaintances with you, if you were gay and single."

"*If* I was gay? How did you not know for sure?" Been a long time since Stratford hadn't set off even the rustiest gaydar.

"I suspected, yeah. But I haven't had a lot of time for dating. Going to a gay club, you don't need to hone that particular skill. Out in the real world, whether a guy was straight or gay didn't matter much. So... Ford. Like the car?"

Like the car. Trust an auto mechanic to see that. "No, like the character in *Hitchhiker's Guide to the Galaxy*."

"Um, what? Is that related to *Doctor Who*?"

Just his luck, to snare a guy without a single geek gene in his body. "It's a book. Sci-fi. By Douglas Adams."

Judging by Vinnie's blank look, the additional explanation wasn't helping any. "I don't mind Stratford at all. Not anymore. When I was younger, it seemed a lot weightier a name, and since I loved sci-fi, I started calling myself Ford. When I met Abby, that's how I introduced myself. She wasn't quite so culturally deficient." Stratford raised an eyebrow, and Vinnie gave him a look that promised retribution.

A split second later Vinnie's fingers were wiggling their way under Stratford's jacket, seeking a particularly heinous tickle-torture retaliation.

Laughing like a maniac and gasping for breath, Stratford was able to slither out of Vinnie's grip before he pissed himself.

"I'm going to regret you ever found out I'm ticklish, aren't I?" Stratford sucked in air between each word.

Vinnie shrugged. "How can you regret something that makes me so happy?"

Hand on hip, Stratford glared. Reaching out a hand, Vinnie tried for him again. Stratford unsuccessfully evaded, but ended up sprawled across Vinnie's lap again.

"No more, please," he begged, only half joking.

"Fine, fine." Vinnie gave a good impression of man denied his deepest, darkest desires before he dipped his head again and dropped a kiss on Stratford's lips. They were both careful not to let it get too hot and heavy, because Vinnie was right. They might be able to live down Stratford's ill-advised words, but there was no way Abby would let them forget if they acted even more like teenagers than they already had.

Vinnie pulled his head back and stared intently into Stratford's eyes.

"I... have something I want to ask."

Butterflies exploded by the millions in Stratford's stomach. Something about Vinnie's intent expression promised good things, but he didn't know what they might be.

"I haven't been with anyone since the minute I saw you. I mean, I hadn't for a while before that, but after I met you, it was because I didn't want to be with anyone else."

"Me neither."

Vinnie's relieved smile told him he'd said the right thing.

"But I want more than that. I want us to be just us."

"Like...." Stratford was almost afraid to say it, afraid the dream was going to pop like a shiny, rainbow-streaked soap bubble. "Like boyfriends."

"Yeah, like boyfriends. Is that... do you want that? With me?"

The dream bubble burst, but it was filled with happiness that seemed to color the whole world. "Yes. Oh, yes."

This time, their kiss was poised to get heated when a loud rumble from Vinnie's midsection interrupted them.

Stratford started laughing. "Guess we should go back in."

"Unless you want me to starve to death, yeah, that's a good idea." Demonstrating just how hungry he was, Vinnie grabbed Stratford's hand and began to gnaw gently on his fingers.

"Stop that." There were a lot of nerve endings in his fingertips, and Vinnie was bringing every one alight, jumpstarting a fire in his groin. Stratford pulled his fingers away and levered himself up from Vinnie's lap. "We're never going to eat if you keep that up."

"Hey, I have an idea. Next time we come over, maybe we could cook one of the dishes we learned about in class."

Although warmed by the notion that Vinnie planned to be around long enough to come to Abby's again, there was one little problem. "Uh, yeah, you might have to do the heavy lifting on that one, Vinnie. I still have to actually complete one class where we don't use my blood as seasoning or without me wearing the main course."

With a noisy smack on his ass, Vinnie propelled Stratford to the door. "Starving. Let's go."

"I CAN'T get enough of you." Vinnie took a break from ravaging Stratford's mouth to speak. Stratford knew exactly what he meant. Defining their relationship had punched his sex drive into poppers and Viagra territory. Staying a respectable length of time at Abby's dinner party, making generic social chitchat with friends he hadn't seen in a while had been nice, but also made him squirm like a kid on Christmas Eve waiting for Santa. Keeping his erection under control had taken up most of his concentration, a fact his friends had continuously teased him about, although thankfully they hadn't known exactly why he'd been so spacey.

"Me neither, but...." Stratford took hold of Vinnie's face and devoured his mouth again. Kissing had never been so addictive. He never wanted to stop, but if they didn't, they'd be coming in their pants again, barely inside Stratford's apartment.

With some effort, he pulled his mouth away from Vinnie's questing tongue.

"Bedroom."

"Okay, okay." Vinnie dragged the words out reluctantly. "I guess if we've got access to a bed, we should use it."

"Yeah. If I've got the chance to get you naked, I'm going to take it."

It wasn't often Vinnie blushed, but when he did, Stratford couldn't get over how special it made him feel. Vinnie was so confident, it amazed him that simple compliments would be enough to turn him bashful, but he'd spoken no more than the truth. Getting Vinnie naked was a treat.

Unable to stop touching each other, they stumbled the short distance to Stratford's bedroom. Stratford felt almost invincible, and he pushed Vinnie back on the bed. Vinnie's legs parted a bit to cradle his hips, and Vinnie reached up to snag the end of Stratford's bow tie, undoing it with a slow, sensuous whisper of fabric against fabric.

Letting his arms drop on the pillow above his head, Vinnie stared up at Stratford, a tender, heated look in his eyes. Stratford grabbed at his untied tie and pulled it off before letting the tip trail across Vinnie's wrist, right by the wooden slat of his headboard.

Vinnie's gaze had followed Stratford's movement, and based on Vinnie's sudden intake of breath, he'd seen the implications of the visual.

"Do it," Vinnie rasped, bucking his hips slightly.

Stratford darted a glance at Vinnie. Somehow, he'd not seen Vinnie as the type who would be content to be tied down, but there was no mistaking the lust and eagerness in his eyes. And it wasn't as though he would tie Vinnie down all that tightly.

With slow, deliberate movements, Stratford used his bow tie to fasten Vinnie's wrist to the headboard. Brushing his hand over Vinnie's chest, he was amazed at the strong, almost frantic thump of Vinnie's heart. There was still no trepidation in Vinnie's gaze when he flicked a glance at his other wrist.

"Got another one?"

Heat rolled through Stratford. His big Italian wasn't seriously asking for another restraint... was he? Vinnie moved his hand to position his wrist right next to the wooden slat and Stratford whimpered.

He grabbed yesterday's tie, which was still lying over the nightstand where he'd tossed it when he undressed the previous night, and amidst a few teasing strokes on the soft skin of Vinnie's inner wrist, he secured his other arm.

For a moment he wondered if he should untie Vinnie to take off his shirt, but then had a mental image of Vinnie lying on his bed, shirt open and splayed, the rest of him completely naked.

That. He wanted that.

Fingers trembling from the effort of not ripping Vinnie's clothes, he arranged Vinnie's shirt the way he wanted. One day, he'd have to ask if Vinnie wore these dress shirts to work because he owned the auto-repair shop, or if he went home and changed before meeting up with Stratford. Not that Stratford cared much either way. The dress shirts were so hot, although he still hoped to have a date with some coveralls and the hood of a car.

He made quick work of Vinnie's pants, and the end result was worth one of those Tumblr posts he sometimes perused, Vinnie's pose debauched and the hard cock with a drop of precum rolling down its length a silent avowal of his need.

"You're gorgeous."

Vinnie's cheeks flushed the way they always did when he complimented the man. But it was nothing less than the truth. He could get off just seeing Vinnie like this.

"And you're wearing too many clothes."

Having one of them naked and the other almost entirely dressed was a game they could play another time. Stratford scrambled off the bed, ready to rip off his clothes as quickly as possible, but something in the way Vinnie stared at him made him change his mind. For the first time in his life, Stratford felt truly cherished and attractive. Vinnie didn't mind that he wasn't a muscle-bound jock. Vinnie had gone and watched *Doctor Who* on his own time because Stratford loved it.

Vinnie's touch was either comforting or arousing, but never once had he ever thought Vinnie disliked touching him. Just the opposite, in fact.

Smirking, he stripped slowly, teasing Vinnie by licking his lips or touching himself. Vinnie tugged against the ties and shifted restlessly. The entire smorgasbord that was Vinnie called to Stratford, from his full lips to his rampant cock to the tips of his feet. When Stratford could stand the craving for Vinnie's skin no longer, he shook off the rest of his clothes and lay full-length along Vinnie's strong, firm body.

The touch of their cocks together had them both groaning.

Vinnie's legs fell open to cradle Stratford, and he settled in to lick, nibble, and tease Vinnie without a care for the time. Neither of them had to work in the morning, and Vinnie was staying the night. If he thought he could last that long without losing his mind, he'd love to tease Vinnie all night long.

After several long minutes that had Vinnie writhing and panting, Stratford came face to face with Vinnie's cock. It was a mouthwatering thing of beauty, unlike that ridiculous Goliath monstrosity.

Reverently, he placed his lips over the domed head, wringing the loudest groan yet from deep within Vinnie's chest. He wrapped one hand around the base and with the other cupped Vinnie's heavy sac. His fingers splayed down along Vinnie's taint, and as soon as Stratford pressed lightly with his middle finger, Vinnie's legs spread even farther apart.

Was that an invitation?

Stratford kept his tongue busy lapping up the precum welling from the tip of Vinnie's sensitive cock but made sure he stared up Vinnie's body to gauge his reaction when he slid his fingers lower. He pressed Vinnie's hole, much as Vinnie had that very first night in the car.

Vinnie's face was flushed, sweaty, and he kept rolling his hips, not to thrust his cock up into Stratford's mouth but to try to capture the finger pushing at his pucker.

This time the begging wasn't wordless. "Fuck me. Dammit, Stratford, please fuck me already."

Stratford had to close his eyes and count to ten... twenty... to keep himself from blowing at Vinnie's desperate yet imperious demand.

Faster than he thought he was capable of, and with no mishaps whatsoever, Stratford grabbed lube and condoms from his bedside table. He quickly rolled on the rubber, to hopefully help desensitize him a little, then slicked Vinnie up. Vinnie's words had made him so crazy he wasn't able to draw out the preparation, because at this point, teasing would only be a cruel torment for them both.

He made himself pause, the head of his cock barely pushing inside, and looked deeply into Vinnie's eyes. Vinnie didn't bother saying anything, only rolled his hips again, and Stratford pushed slowly home.

Stratford pulled almost all the way out, then sank back in, a little harder, a little faster. Vinnie's body started to shake, and he was sucking in air like a bellows.

Concerned, Stratford paused.

"Don't fucking stop," Vinnie snarled at him, and suddenly Vinnie's expression became recognizable. Vinnie was seconds from coming, and the knowledge pushed Stratford right to the brink. He thrust inside, hard and fast, four more times before Vinnie's hands tightened into fists, the skin whitening around the bow-tie restraints, and his thighs shook around Stratford. The pale streaks painting Vinnie's chest and the rhythmic clench of the passage around Stratford's cock sent his own explosion jettisoning into the condom.

Their bodies twitched with involuntary shakes for several long moments after Stratford slumped boneless against Vinnie, uncaring that he was smearing cum between them.

Once they'd gotten their breath back, Stratford slid carefully out of Vinnie. Before he stripped off the condom or went to look for a cloth or T-shirt to wipe them off, he loosened the ties at Vinnie's wrists. Vinnie grabbed him, engulfing him in arms that hadn't touched him in far too long, and pressed kisses along his neck and jaw before landing on Stratford's lips.

He hadn't been lying when he told Vinnie it didn't matter to him if they never got around to anal sex. But Vinnie's trust, Vinnie's openness while they were engaging in it... that was special, and he wasn't sure how long it would have taken him to become aware of it if they hadn't taken this step.

This contentment, the sensation of having someone there who'd have your back.... This is what everyone was searching for, and Stratford hadn't even known. Some wild twist of fate had given him this gift, a man who would undoubtedly become the partner he'd always dreamed of, and he was more grateful than he could express.

Vinnie kissed him until their chest hairs began to stick together, and Stratford laughingly separated them.

"I'm cleaning us up. We've got all night for kissing or whatever."

"I'll take a couple of helpings of whatever and a side of kissing."

Stratford rolled his eyes and squeaked when Vinnie gave his butt an unexpected slap. He tried to glare at Vinnie, but it was impossible when he was trying not to laugh. "Um, excuse me, but butt slapping is clearly shenanigans, not whatever."

Vinnie laughed too, but his words were serious. "I'll take whatever's on your menu, Stratford. Anything and everything."

Stratford's eyes burned, just a bit, at the declaration, and he hauled ass for the bathroom to grab a towel so they could explore the menu some more. He had the best boyfriend ever.

Eleven

STRATFORD stared for a moment at Vinnie's big Navigator parked across from the entrance to his apartment. He'd given Vinnie a key only the past weekend, exactly one week after they officially became exclusive. Yesterday he'd been thrilled to come home and find Vinnie waiting for him, with food he'd magically whipped up in his half-assed kitchen. Best Monday he'd had in a long fucking time. Then they'd spent a long time fucking, making it an even better day.

Today, though? He had a feeling Vinnie was going to want to return it. Sure, they were boyfriends, but they hadn't discussed the L word. Too soon for Vinnie, even though Stratford was sure he'd fallen in love weeks ago. Better this way, though. Vinnie would be better cutting his loses and running, because Stratford was a giant fucking loser, and if he'd admitted to being in love, he'd only be that much more pathetic.

Upstairs, Marley ignored him, and the scent of dinner made him nauseous.

"Mmm, you're finally home." Vinnie finished whatever arcane task he was performing at the counter before he turned and came to greet Stratford.

"Holy shit, what happened?"

Stratford stared up at the ceiling. He wasn't even sure he knew what happened. Or at least, why it had happened.

"I got fired." A week before Christmas. Fired. He wanted to throw up.

"Fired?" Vinnie flipped a switch to turn off the hot plate and gathered Stratford in his arms, taking him to the bedroom.

But this wasn't an injured hand or a cramped limb. Vinnie wasn't going to be able to fix this, and as soon as his shock wore off, he'd realize there were a million better prospects than Stratford out there.

"What happened?" Vinnie rubbed his back in an attempt to soothe him, but it didn't work.

"I honestly don't know. About three this afternoon, Gonzalez called me into his office and told me my work was filled with errors and I was done."

A hot tear streaked down his face. "I made a typo a couple of weeks ago, but it was all fixed before anything went to print. Why would they fire me now over that?"

"Um, three o'clock?"

"Yeah, I wandered around for a couple of hours. I didn't know… what to do."

He was no longer Doctor Chicken. For so long, he'd hated being Doctor Chicken, but now he was strangely bereft. And the likelihood of anyone responding to his résumés this close to Christmas was… slim. People just didn't hire around the holidays. Not for office jobs, anyway.

The numbness in his fingers might be frostbite or it might be shock. He didn't know, and he wasn't sure it was important.

"You said three o'clock?"

Why was the time so important? He really looked at Vinnie for the first time since he got home. The man was pale. Paler than Stratford had ever seen.

"Are you okay?"

Vinnie bit his lip and stood up to start pacing. Here it came. Vinnie was going tell him they shouldn't see each other anymore.

"I think…. Look. A couple of weeks ago, I had my sister look into the finances at Nectar."

Stratford blinked as he tried to make sense of the last words he expected to hear.

"Why?"

Vinnie glanced at him a moment, but then he continued pacing and talking.

"I'd thought maybe they weren't compensating you because they were having financial difficulty or something, and if they were, I was going to warn you so you could find another job, at the very least."

"And?"

"They were fine. In excellent shape, actually. So I made an appointment with the owner of the company."

The chill in Stratford's fingers migrated to his gut. He had an inkling maybe getting fired wasn't going to be the worst of his day.

"Why exactly would my boss's boss even take such a meeting?"

"Er, well, sometimes business owners will meet with other business owners. Potential for networking."

There was something fishy about this, and it wasn't whatever Vinnie had been cooking.

"The owner of Nectar Greeting Cards & Gifts wanted to network with the owner of an auto-repair shop." Stratford's voice was flat. He certainly didn't want to disparage Vinnie's worth, but Nectar's owner was an even greedier asshole than Gonzalez.

Vinnie's cheeks flushed, as guilty as a kid who'd thrown a ball through a window.

"So, yes, I own an auto-repair shop. I worked there all through high school and for a few years after, but shortly after my dad died, I came up with a modification to an existing tool and from that managed to, um, start a business that manufactures tools for auto mechanics."

Stratford tilted his head. He still wasn't sure he had all the pieces of the puzzle in front of him because clearly the Vinnie he thought he'd known was a mirage.

"I can only assume it's a big…." Oh. Even he'd heard of Vinnie's company. They had billboards along the industrial complexes with a bunch of clustered auto shops. "Stupid of me. Giani Tools?"

He'd never seen anyone look so embarrassed to admit to success, but then, Vinnie wasn't exactly admitting to success here, he was getting caught in a lie. Stratford rarely got angry, but he sensed it building, melting the ice in his chest and limbs and replacing it with a seething mass of lava, ready to explode.

The final piece of the puzzle dropped in with the finality of a coffin lid slamming down. "When was your meeting at Nectar?"

"I'm so sorry, Stratford. After we chatted for a bit, I mentioned I thought you should be getting a percentage of—"

Stratford held out a palm to halt the flow of words. "When was your meeting?"

"Today at two thirty."

The silence after Vinnie's announcement was deafening. Until Stratford shouted, sending Marley skittering beneath the bed to cower.

"What the fuck, Vinnie? You lied to me and got me fired. And for what? Because you wanted to control my life?"

"No, but you weren't asking for what you deserved...."

"Jesus fucking Christ, Vinnie. You own a hugely successful business. I stupidly signed away my rights. Even I know that business isn't always fucking fair. So should you."

"I would never treat my employees like that."

Stratford wanted to throw something, but he didn't have enough actual things he could afford to break. He'd feared the whole relationship was too good to be true, and sadly, he was right. Instead, he sneered. "Well good for you. But guess what? Some places aren't as great to work at, but that doesn't give you the right to go in and talk to my boss's boss like you were having a parent-teacher conference discussing the bullying of your child. This is my life and you didn't even ask!"

"I'm sorry, I'll go back—"

"You will fucking not. This is my problem, not yours."

"No, it's our problem. We should be facing problems together."

"Do you even hear what you're saying? Just hours after you went behind my back to try to solve my problem for me? I can stand on my own two feet, you know. I've been doing it for a long time."

Stratford had no idea where this cold, logical calm had come from. It was a thin, brittle crust over the seething mass of his emotions, and he didn't know when it would fracture.

"I know, but I also know you don't like confrontation, so I thought...."

"You thought you'd be doing me a favor. This was a problem that we didn't need to face together. You were just going to wave your magic wand and make my life better. Well, you failed. I don't have a job, and I'm going to get kicked out of my apartment. Good work, Vinnie."

Vinnie flinched as though he'd taken a paring knife and carved the words in his flesh, and he stretched out a hand to touch Stratford, but Stratford launched himself off the bed to evade it. If Vinnie touched him, he was going to fucking lose it.

"You don't have to worry about that. I can cover your rent. Or we can get you a bigger apartment. I don't mind paying for it. I can afford it."

"Of course you can afford it. You own Giani Tools. But tell me… why did you lie about that?"

The flush, which hadn't really receded, got darker. "I know it's no excuse, but so many guys—and women—have wanted to date me for my money."

A bitter laugh welled up in Stratford's throat. "I thought so. But now, suddenly it's okay if I want your money? Or is it because I'm a pathetic charity case who can't manage his own fucking life?"

"No, I meant to tell you."

"When? When we'd been dating a year? Ten years? Was it supposed to be my Christmas present?" Stratford didn't think he'd ever heard himself use such a poisonous tone, but he knew where he'd picked it up. His mother's last words to him had sliced with the same venomous blade. It made him sick to know he'd reverted to her example, but he couldn't stop the words rolling from his tongue.

"You need to leave."

The blood drained from Vinnie's face. "Stratford, no. Please. I'm so sorry. I shouldn't have done it, I know, but we can work it out."

"No, I don't think we can, Vinnie. There is no 'we' in this equation. No partnership. Clearly there never was."

Vinnie shook his head and stepped forward, hands shifting as if he wanted to touch Stratford but was afraid of another dodge.

"I'm so, so sorry Stratford. If I could do it all over again, I would."

"I know you think I need to stand up for myself, and that's what I'm doing. Get out." Vinnie didn't move. "We're done. Vincent."

The simple act of using Vinnie's full name seemed to push the comprehension home.

"I love you, Stratford. Please don't do this."

Stratford bit back a flippant "whatever" and stood impassively while Vinnie left the apartment. As soon as he heard the door at the bottom of the stairs close, he dropped back on his bed. Marley jumped up beside him and he picked her up.

Her unconditional loving warmth was all it took to break the ice over his sorrow. He wasn't sure what was worse, losing the man he loved or realizing how little that man respected him. The first time Vinnie had said he loved Stratford would also be the last. Too bad he couldn't believe Vinnie was telling the truth. Stratford broke into loud, noisy sobs, burying his face in Marley's fur.

VINNIE sat in his car, engine running. The minutes, blurred by the tears that kept welling in his eyes, ticked by. After twenty of them had passed, the collar of his shirt was wet, and he had to accept that Stratford wasn't going to chase him down, tell him he'd changed his mind about the finality of ending their relationship. Vinnie fingered the new silvery keys hanging alongside his house keys. He'd never been more pleased or proud to accept a gift as when Stratford had handed him a copy of keys to his apartment. He probably should have returned them, but he couldn't bear to. Giving them back meant there was no hope, and he couldn't live with that.

He'd never been in love before, and he couldn't believe Stratford didn't love him back. Love had to be enough to make things work. It had to.

Another ten minutes rolled by with no Stratford, no call, no nothing. Vinnie grabbed some napkins from the glove box and scrubbed at his face. His nose was sore and swollen, and a headache pulsed angrily in his temples, but it was no more than he deserved. The tears wouldn't stop, but he put the car into gear anyway.

Turning onto his street, Vinnie pulled into an unfamiliar driveway ten houses down from where his family lived. The sweet little red-brick three-bedroom bungalow that was supposed to have been Stratford's Christmas present, the start of their lives together. When Stratford had so snidely asked if the truth was to be his present, well, it had been.

He'd been going to confess about his company and ask Stratford to move in with him. How had he managed to screw up so badly?

He didn't know what he was going to do with the house now. There wasn't any point in leaving his family just for the sake of leaving. He stared at the house, remembering how he'd been able to see him and Stratford together in each room. But would Stratford have even seen it for the gift he'd intended?

Unable to look at the cute little house any longer, he rested his head against the steering wheel and cried as he hadn't done since his dad's funeral.

ACHY and stuffed up but finally dry-eyed, Stratford wrote a note to his landlord, packed his clothes, laptop, and sketchbooks into a large suitcase, shoved Marley into a carrier, and headed to the bus without a backwards glance.

Two-and-a-half hours after he cut his own heart out, Stratford stood on Abby's doorstep with all of his most important worldly possessions sitting beside him on the concrete. He refused to look at the porch rocker where he and Vinnie had agreed to be exclusive. With a trembling finger, he reached out and rang the doorbell.

Feet pounded toward the door, and Abby flung the door open.

"Stratford?"

"Hi Abby. I think I need some help." The tears he thought he'd finished crying came back with a vengeance as Abby pulled him into a hug.

"I'D LIKE you home tomorrow for dinner." His mama's tone indicated she wouldn't accept any argument. Vinnie's eyes burned, because it wasn't as though he'd have anything else to do on a Saturday night. Not anymore. The gaping emptiness of his life without Stratford stretched endlessly before him. All he did was go to work, lock himself in his office, and refuse to take meetings. He'd obsessively check his phone for messages when he wasn't leaving ones on Stratford's. It had been three days of complete radio silence. Five more days until

Christmas. He had no idea how he was going to pretend everything was okay.

Nevertheless, his mother's demand sounded oddly foreboding and gave him something to think about beside his own misery.

"Uh, okay. Is something wrong?"

His mother did something he didn't think he'd ever seen. She giggled and tucked a lock of still-black hair behind her ear. Vinnie leaned back and inspected his mom closely. For so many years she'd been his mom, even if they'd spent many of the intervening years raising his sisters. Now, he saw a rosy flush on her cheeks that may or may not have been the result of makeup. The darkened lashes, hint of eye shadow and pinked lips were definitely the result of makeup. His mother rarely bothered.

"I have someone to introduce to the family."

Vinnie's breath froze in his lungs. "What do you mean?"

"I've been seeing someone. Stanos Andronov. He owns the organic butcher's on Hutchison."

"Seeing someone?" He could barely string together a coherent sentence. It had never once occurred to him that his mother would date someone. Ever.

"Yes. He's a wonderful man. And it's time."

"Time? Yes, when have you had time to date someone?"

His mother laughed in that way that reminded him of being a kid again, that mocking hint of "mother knows best."

"Vinnie. You've been a busy man for a long time. Your sisters are self-sufficient and busy with their own lives. Sienna's in school half the day. I have lots of time for dating. You've just never been around to see it."

"What are you going to tell the girls?"

She laughed again. "They all know. You're the last one I've told, and that's because I didn't want to upset you until it was serious."

"And it's serious? He's serious?"

"Yes, it is, Vinnie. I want you to meet him. I want you to give him a chance. He's not going to be replacing your father. But it's time. It's past time. We're talking about getting married."

"Married! How can you possibly talk about getting married? We've worked so hard, and if I've got to wait until Evie's in college before I start living, you need to wait too."

Never mind that he'd been planning to start a little early. Considering he'd bought a house so close, he thought he'd be near enough if they needed him, but if his mother was moving on.... Didn't matter. Those plans were in ashes, and all he had now was his family.

His mother narrowed her eyes. "*Mi caro*, I'm not your kid or one of your sisters. I'm your mama. You've done right by your family. I wouldn't have made it through without you, and I'm more thankful than I can say. Between helping me and raising your sisters, you even found time to start your company, creating something bigger and better than the shop. I am so proud of you. But our job is done. Now. Not in a few years.

"Marissa has her fancy degree and a great job with your company. Gabriella's man loves her and Sienna. I wouldn't be surprised if he proposed as soon as she graduates. Evie's off to college next year. It's time for you and me to find something besides raising kids, because that job is done. I will always love your father, but I love Stanos too, and I know I can be happy with him. You are smart, resourceful, and so full of love—Stratford is a lucky man, but you can't expect him to wait for some arbitrary date to arrive so you can *start living*."

The knowledge that his mom had found someone, that their family would be irrevocably changing, broke the fragile hold he had on his emotions. He wanted to run to Stratford, seek comfort in his arms, but he'd lost that right.

"Mama, Stratford broke up with me." Again, Vinnie's eyes burned with tears, a sensation he'd become more familiar with than he'd like over the past couple of days. "I... I've lost him."

His mother ceased being an independent woman with her own love life, ceased being the woman he'd shared responsibility of the household with for fifteen years, and became simply his mom. She gave him a big hug.

"What happened?"

None of the things he'd done had seemed like bad plans at the time. But Stratford's reaction and his mom's pursed lips as he recounted their fight had him second-guessing himself in a way he hadn't in years.

As she had countless times for scraped knees and bumped chins, she wiped his wet face with her thumbs and kissed him lightly on both cheeks.

"Love can make us stupid, my son. But I think you can get him back. You're one of the most determined men I've ever met—you always have been. Your Stratford has made you happier than I've seen you in many, many years. He's what you need, as long as you remember he's your man and not a child you're responsible for. A partner, perhaps one day a husband. An equal partnership, not the unequal power balance you needed to maintain while your sisters were young. I may have been a stay-at-home mom, but don't think for one minute your father and I didn't make big decisions together, after discussing things."

Vinnie nodded. His mother was a strong woman, but he'd somehow managed to treat his boyfriend the way he treated his sisters when they were growing up, like he wanted to keep them in a bubble to protect them from all harm. The sentiment wasn't bad, but making decisions for Stratford hadn't been fair to either of them. How could he convince Stratford of that if he wouldn't even take his calls?

"But I'm still your mama, and this is still my house, which means some decisions are mine alone. If you think I'm living here with you after I get married, you are quite mistaken. There isn't enough room to add both Stratford and Stanos to this house."

"Are you kicking me out?" Although she seemed to be telling him he should move in with Stratford. Or something. If he could get Stratford back.

"If that's what it takes. Time to leave the nest. That's what happens. Your sisters will be here for a bit, but you can give them the support they need without being here all the time."

"How do you know they'll be okay? How do you know I can fix things with Stratford?"

"How do I know? I always know. I know because I raised you right. I know because you've given so much of yourself for your family for so long. You're a good man, and if I raised the best son, that must mean I'm the best, smartest mama that ever lived."

Vinnie let out a watery chuckle.

His mom patted him on the hand. "Now, *mi caro*, a little bird told me the house down the street was sold. I know you were thinking of your old mama when you bought it. Just because you have to leave the nest doesn't mean I want you to go far."

He kissed his mom and stood. He wasn't going to give up on Stratford. He couldn't.

THE next day, Vinnie stood on Abby's porch as snow swirled around his feet. He'd already been by Stratford's apartment, using his keys to get in when Stratford didn't answer the buzzer. He'd panicked when he saw Marley was missing, along with Stratford's sketches. If Stratford wasn't here... well, if he wasn't here, Abby would just have to tell him where to find Stratford.

He took a deep breath and rang the bell.

A few moments later, Abby swung the door open.

"Took you long enough."

"Um, what? I've been calling almost nonstop, but it just goes to voice mail."

Abby shook her head. "I don't think he's had his phone on since he got here. But you made a right mess of things, Vince."

He hung his head. "I know. But Abby, I love him. I was an idiot, and... and...." His eyes did that stupid burning thing again, but he didn't think breaking down on Abby's porch would work in his favor.

"Look, I think I've got him to the point where he'll at least listen to you. But don't do anything stupid like this again." She looked at the parcels in his hand. "Coming armed. Not a bad idea. Follow me."

Abby left him outside a room that had a television playing some cartoon he didn't recognize. The tousled brown hair visible over the high arm of the couch was recognizable.

He swallowed and stepped into the room.

"Not watching the Doctor?"

Stratford let out a bleat of surprise and scrambled back against the far arm of the couch. Marley, startled by the sudden movement, thudded to the floor and waddled past Vinnie. Even though Stratford looked wan and worn out, he was exactly perfect in Vinnie's eyes.

"Wha—" Stratford's voice cracked and he cleared his throat before speaking again. "What are you doing here?"

"To talk. First, though, I brought you some things."

"Why? More things to buy me off?" Stratford frowned, but the heat of their earlier argument was absent. He merely sounded sad.

"No." Vinnie didn't know if this was the right thing, but if Stratford was hurting as bad as he was, they had to be able to get past this. Vinnie handed Stratford a cardboard cup with a latte from his favorite cafe, then began pulling items out of his bags.

"Homemade manicotti, like the kind I made the first night I saw you. If your last few days have been like mine, you probably haven't been eating much." Food had never had such little appeal to him.

"But we made pad Thai at our first cooking class."

Vinnie let himself smile. "I told you I saw a guy with a bow tie outside the window that night you were watching. What I didn't tell you was that I ran outside after you. Fate must have been working even then."

"Fate?" Stratford raised an eyebrow.

"Fate, luck, destiny. Whatever it was that led you to me started working that night."

Stratford's lower lip trembled, and he made a point of trying to peer into Vinnie's bags.

"A cinnamon bun and a white-chocolate scone, both from your favorite cafe. The wine we had for our first dinner date."

He reached down to the bottom for the fuzzy mouse. "A catnip toy for Marley."

His heart skipped a beat when Stratford chuckled, and the kernel of hope in his heart sprouted.

With a final flourish, he pulled out a florist box. "And a dozen red roses."

"Roses? When did we ever have roses?"

Vinnie shrugged. "It's the universal language of apologies. And love."

Stratford dropped his gaze, but Vinnie was close, he was sure of it. He sat on the couch, crowding Stratford a bit, and reached out for his hand.

He stroked Stratford's chilly fingers gently and spoke. He'd only get one chance at this, and he had to get it right.

"I wasn't lying. I love you. I know it's quick, but it's true. You make me happier than I've ever been, and I can't picture my life without you. I don't want to. I handled the whole job thing badly, and I shouldn't have lied to you. It was stupid of me. Please, please give me a chance to make this up to you."

Stratford's fingers curled around his for just a second.

"Vinnie, I...."

"Please, Stratford."

"I've talked to Abby about this until my throat hurt, but she helped me see that maybe I was being a little unfair. You've spent years taking care of your family, and you took on that responsibility at a very young age. I get that it's maybe natural for you to take charge like you did. I had seen signs of it here and there, but it never occurred to me you'd...."

"Treat you like my kid?"

Stratford nodded and picked at the hem of his pajama top with the hand not in Vinnie's.

"I'm so sorry. I'll work on that, I promise."

"If we're going to be together, you can't do that."

Vinnie's hope grew a few more tendrils.

"And about lying to me...." Stratford didn't finish his sentence, but Vinnie was confident he knew the right answer.

"Never again. I swear."

Stratford cracked a sheepish smile. "I understand that too. Once Abby told me what your company is worth. But I never cared if you had money."

"I know, believe me, I knew right from the first day, in my gut and heart, but my head told me to be careful, and I listened to it."

"I need to tell you, I kept something from you too. Thanksgiving weekend, I sent out a bunch of résumés. I knew you and Abby were right. They were treating me like shit at Nectar, and it was time to cut my losses and go. I didn't want to tell you because... because.... I don't really have a good reason. I was scared to think about leaving what I'd known for so long."

Vinnie slid a little closer, and Stratford resettled his legs so they rested over Vinnie's thighs. Just that little bit of contact made the tension in his shoulders ease up for the first time in days.

"It's okay. Going forward, no more lies, right?"

"Right. And we'll make decisions together. I want a partner, not a babysitter."

Ouch. But he still had one more thing to confess.

"So, I got you one more thing." Vinnie pulled a tiny flat box from his pocket. "And if you don't want it, I'll understand. But I bought it... because I wanted to surprise you. I want to make you happy. And I want, more than anything, to be with you always. It's a big decision, one I made without talking to you. When you talked about getting the truth on Christmas, I had actually been planning to tell you about my company because that's the only way I could explain your gift."

Stratford stared at him, confusion filling his eyes.

Vinnie handed him the box. "I got you fireplaces."

Opening the box, Stratford pulled out a set of keys. "What are these?"

"I sort of bought a house. With fireplaces. And if you don't want to live there now, or live there ever, it's okay. I can give it to one of my sisters when they get married, but don't, please don't...." Vinnie ran out of words, because if Stratford wanted to kick him to the curb for this, no words would stop that.

Stratford curled his hand around the keys for a moment before he put them back in the box and handed it back to Vinnie.

Hope died in Vinnie's chest, and he couldn't catch his breath.

"You hang on to this."

"What?"

"I have a good feeling about some of those jobs I applied for. When I have a new job and can contribute to expenses, we'll revisit the fireplaces."

Vinnie wasn't quite sure what was happening. "But, but...."

"I've struggled to keep on my own two feet for almost as long as you've been the father figure in your family. It's not a habit that will easily go away, but if I'm going to ask you to break your habit of making decisions all by yourself, then I have to try to let you help me. I'll stay here until I get a job, and we can make sure we're building a good foundation for our relationship. If you want, I will let you help out with my expenses."

Relief flooded Vinnie, and somewhat alarmingly, stiffened his cock to full mast in his jeans.

"Then, are we… good?"

"We're good. I love you, Vinnie."

Vinnie groaned. His cock knew what was going on better than his brain. He fell back on the couch, bringing Stratford with him.

The second their lips met lust exploded between them, and they devoured each other's mouth as their hands sought bare skin.

"Hey, hey, hey." Abby's voice was like a bucket of cold water, and Stratford rolled off him onto the floor in his surprise.

"Abby, what the hell?" Stratford's response was far different than when Vinnie's mother had surprised them, and Vinnie much preferred this.

"This is why you've got a guest room, Stratford. Go make up in there."

Vinnie laughed, and Stratford grabbed his hand, guiding him past Abby.

Stratford pushed him back on the bed, but before Stratford pounced, Vinnie spoke.

"I have one more question. Do you have plans for Christmas?"

A sweet, sexy smile stretched Stratford's lips. "Yes. I'll be at your place, meeting your family."

"Damn right you will." Vinnie pulled him down and glanced at the headboard. "Did you bring any bow ties with you?"